SUNNY SIDE UP . . .

Longarm looked back at Breed.

The man was sitting on the ground holding his guts in both hands. He was trying to push them back in through the bloody hole in his pants. They were sleek, glistening gray coils flecked with blood, and with each breath Breed took, they surged relentlessly out past his filthy, clutching fingers. Considering how long a man's guts were, pushing them back in was a near impossible assignment, and besides, Breed was in no condition to handle t

Tears in his eyes, Breed lo

"My God! Look

"Don't feel bad."

"Why not?"

"There's plenty of buzzards out here looking for a good meal . . ."

*Also in the LONGARM series
from Jove*

→← TABOR EVANS →←

LONGARM

AND THE
SKULL CANYON GANG

JOVE BOOKS, NEW YORK

LONGARM AND THE SKULL CANYON GANG

A Jove Book / published by arrangement with
the author

PRINTING HISTORY
Jove edition / June 1991

ISBN: 0-515-10597-X

Jove Books are published by The Berkley Publishing Group,
200 Madison Avenue, New York, New York 10016.
The name "JOVE" and the "J" logo
are trademarks belonging to Jove Publications, Inc.

PRINTED IN THE UNITED STATES OF AMERICA

10 9 8 7 6 5 4 3 2 1

LONGARM

AND THE
SKULL CANYON GANG

Chapter 1

Longarm was certain. These two scum he was watching had to be members of the gang Vail had sent him after.

The two men looked like they'd crawled out from under a rock, a particularly damp and noxious one, at that. The short one was a squat, gnomelike creature who spoke in a kind of snarl, a curse always ready on his lips. He wore a filthy derby hat, a torn sheepskin coat, and tattered Levi's. His unshaven face had a caked mask of dust and grime, as much a part of him as his dirty, droopy ears and snarled hair.

His companion, almost comically tall in comparison, had a crazed, unsettling look in his eyes as he peered about him—so that even when he reached out for the coffeepot, the move had menace in it. He was like a steam engine that could not be throttled down. Watching him tend the horses a moment ago, Longarm had noted his quick, rough movements and the unfeeling cruelty with which he handled the animals, especially when he led them off to graze near the stream below the camp.

They were eating supper at the moment. Less than twenty yards away behind a screen of pine, Longarm had no difficulty hearing them wolf down their food. Perched on two logs close by the fire, they were bent close over their tin plates as they shoveled the beans and bacon into their gaunt faces with short, snoutish grunts, a uniquely gluttonous chorus.

Longarm had followed them from Rim Rock, more certain with each mile he covered that at long last he had overtaken members of the gang that had caused the disappearance of two federal marshals and, most recently, a Pinkerton. A mile back they had raided a settler's cabin, shooting the settler down in cold blood. Before riding off with their booty, they had set fire to his cabin. Had Longarm not been tailing them, there would have been no witness to their crime. As it was, Longarm was not happy that he had not been close enough or fast enough to intervene. Though it would have been his one gun against their two, it was a match he would have relished.

Now they were within reach.

Only Longarm had a problem: Should he take these lice in now or keep on their tail and let them lead him to the rest of the gang? After a moment he decided that since he could not be sure these two *would* lead him to the gang, he had better take them in now while they were within reach. Perhaps once they were in custody they might be persuaded to cooperate with Longarm in tracking the Skull Canyon Gang.

Longarm reached across his waist and withdrew his .44-40 double-action Colt from its cross-draw rig, then moved back out of the pines, a man so tall the crown of his hat brushed a branch better than six feet off the ground. Once clear of the pines, he stepped into view. The two men caught the movement and turned swiftly to face him. The taller one flung aside his tin plate and jumped to his feet. His companion remained seated on the log.

"Don't go for your guns," Longarm said as he walked toward them.

"Put away that iron, stranger," the short one said. "You don't need it. If it's coffee and grub you want, we got plenty of both."

"You guessed wrong."

"You got no call to draw down on us," the tall one said. "Can't you see we ain't packin' no iron?"

As he spoke he edged back to get the campfire's blaze between him and Longarm. Longarm stepped quickly closer to him, leveling his gun on his chest.

"Stand right where you are," he told him.

The man held up, a grin cracking his mean, wolfish face. "Why're you so nervous, you son of a bitch? You're the one got the gun."

"Don't rile him, Ely," said the short stocky fellow still sitting on the log. "You want him to get mean and start pullin' that trigger?"

"He hasn't got the guts to squeeze it."

The short one sniggered. "Oh, my, you're right. He's afraid it might go off."

"Come on, mister," Ely cajoled, half serious, "put away the gun. Join us for a smoke."

"Hey, mister, we got some beans left," said the other one.

"Turn around, Ely," Longarm said. "I want your back to me."

3

"You going to shoot me in the back?"

"Do it."

Slowly, Ely turned his back on Longarm. Longarm looked over at the smaller one. He was peering up at Longarm from the log, his porcine face revealing a feral eagerness, as if he were enjoying every moment of this unexpected confrontation.

"You too, Fatty," Longarm said. "Get off that log and get over by your partner."

"Don't call me Fatty, you son of a bitch. I don't like it. Name's Smith, Windy Smith."

Longarm waggled his gun at him. "Stand up."

"You goin' to kill us?"

"You reckon I got a reason to want to?"

"Maybe he's kin to that settler we stomped back there," said Ely.

"That so?" Windy asked Longarm.

"No, but I saw what you two done."

The tall one turned half around to address Longarm. "Hey, listen, mister. That weren't no fault of ours. That crazy sodbuster went for his iron."

Longarm did not care to argue the point.

"Get off that log, Windy," he said once again, "or I'll wrap this barrel around your head."

"I'm scared," cried Windy, giggling. "Oh, my God, here I am confronting Fearless Ned, the mean killer what captured the Railroad Gang."

Longarm bent to rap Smith just as Smith's hand swung up sharply with one end of a half-consumed piece of firewood. The branch was as thick and round as a man's arm. As Longarm jumped back, it caught his wrist a numbing blow, sending his weapon spinning into the

4

deep grass beyond the fire. Longarm broke back. The taller one lunged after him and knocked him to the ground. Before Longarm could scramble back up onto his feet, Windy was upon him, battering him ferociously about the head and shoulders with his club until Ely, his crazed eyes gleaming, snatched it from him and continued the punishment. Long after Longarm lost consciousness the man kept on beating him with a frenzied, mad fury.

Longarm awoke, shivering violently. A glance at the stars told him it was close to dawn. It took a conscious effort on his part to get control of his trembling limbs. His head pounded unmercifully and when he put his hand up to it, he felt the blood caking his hair, both on the crown of his head and just above his right temple. His left shoulder was bruised considerably as well, but he could still get his arm to work for him. His head was another matter. Whenever he moved his head too quickly, he got the weird impression his skull was a cracked eggshell—and leaking badly.

He fumbled about in the grass until he found his hat, then got up carefully, his balance so bad it felt as if he were at the end of all-night bender. He weaved over to the grassy spot to look for his Colt, but couldn't find it, and was about to give it up as an impossible task when the toe of his right boot kicked it. He bent carefully, retrieved the weapon, then walked back past the pines for his mount, a big chestnut gelding he'd hired in Rim Rock.

By the time he reached it, the pounding in his head was a continuous roar. He had to squint to see. Climbing

5

onto the horse was a prolonged agony, but he managed somehow. By mid-afternoon he was still in the saddle. But only just barely. Feverish, he had long since drained what water remained in his canteen. When a little after dusk he caught sight ahead of him of a green line of cottonwoods and willows, it seemed nothing short of a miracle. He straightened in his saddle and kept on doggedly toward the trees.

When he reached them, he found them a fragrant Eden of cool shade. The stream that watered them still flowed, despite the long hot dry summer. He eased himself off the chestnut, staggered to the bank of the stream, and flinging off his hat, plunged his head and shoulders facedown into the icy water. Amazingly refreshed, he filled the crown of his hat with water, drank deep from it, then set the hat back down on his head, letting what water remained stream down over his head and shoulders. In the shallows a few yards farther down, his horse was drinking its fill and doing so sensibly. As Longarm glanced at it, the chestnut lifted its dripping muzzle from the stream and returned Longarm's glance, flicking its ears—as if to say, "Oh, hell, I was sure waitin' for that."

Night had fallen by then. He reckoned he was only ten miles or so from Iron City, and was thinking he could make it before midnight. He got to his feet, still woozy but immensely refreshed, and started for his horse to get the canteen hanging from his saddlehorn. He would need to fill it before riding on. Lifting the rawhide loop over the saddlehorn, he took it to the stream, unscrewed the cap, and bent low over the water. He lost his balance and almost plunged, fully clothed, into the water before sprawling on the grass beside the stream. He hung on grimly as the world spun sickeningly around him. The moment he had ducked his head, it had exploded on him, and now he could barely see through the tiny, exploding pinpoints of light that danced before his eyes.

He took a deep breath and carefully reached into the stream with the canteen. Once it was heavy with the icy water, he sat up carefully on the bank to screw the cap tight. As he did so, he felt rather than heard the presence of someone behind him. He turned. A man he had never seen before was covering him with a Navy Colt. The stranger was wearing a black, flat-crowned plainsman's hat and a buttonless leather vest over a white shirt. His lean face was grim, his dark eyes gleaming with determination. Over his right shoulder was slung a bulging saddlebag.

"Sorry, mister," he said, "but I'm a long way from home. And I need your mount—and that canteen."

He reached down swiftly and took the canteen from Longarm, then turned and dropped its rawhide loop over the chestnut's saddlehorn. With the man's back to him, Longarm drew his .44, but he had become so feeble that the moment the revolver cleared its holster, it dropped from his grasp. At the sound of the Colt thumping to the ground, the stranger whirled about and cocked his own weapon.

Then he saw Longarm's .44 in the grass beside him. Chuckling, he swept it up and flung it into the trees.

"You'll be all right, mister," he told Longarm, as he swung up onto the chestnut. "This here's a regular stop for them headin' into the hills yonder. And you got plenty of water here."

7

"Don't take that horse," Longarm managed, his mouth as dry as pasteboard.

"It's a handsome brute, I admit. But I need it, stranger. This ain't personal, you understand. And I'm right sorry I have to do this. But I'm a long way from home and I got no choice in the matter."

Longarm grabbed for the derringer in his watch-fob pocket, but even as he managed to claw it free and unclip it, the trees spun crazily about his head and this weapon too fell from his enfeebled grasp. His supporting left arm gave way then, and he collapsed facedown onto the damp grass, tried to raise his head, but found he no longer had enough strength to accomplish even that.

He heard the saddle leather creak under the stranger's weight, and expected to hear next the sudden beat of the chestnut's hooves as the man galloped off. Instead, he heard the man dismount. A moment later, on one knee beside him, the stranger rolled Longarm gently over onto his back, then placed his hand under the back of Longarm's head and lifted gently. Longarm felt the neck of the canteen being thrust past his cracked lips, then the cool trickle of icy water across his tongue and down his throat.

He opened his eyes and squinted through the fiery pinpoints of light at the stranger bent over him. He was frowning down at Longarm, concern evident in his dark eyes.

"My name's Wells, Jim Wells," he said. "What's your handle, mister?"

"Custis Long."

"Well, Custis," Wells said, "I was so blamed anxious

to get hold of your horse, I didn't notice how bad off you were."

Longarm said nothing. The task of conversing was too difficult for him. He felt himself beginning to shiver uncontrollably. The stranger bent close to examine him.

"What happened? Fall off your horse?"

Longarm summoned all his strength and managed to tell him about the two riders he had seen rob and kill the settler, then burn his place down, and how badly he had bungled his attempt to collar them. He did not mention that he was a U.S. deputy marshal.

"There ain't no holes in you," Wells commented when Longarm finished. "Where'd they get you?"

"Last thing I remember, they were beating me about the head and shoulders. They were very enthusiastic." By now Longarm was talking through clenched teeth as he tried to halt their chattering.

"Looks like you got a head injury," Wells said, peering closely at the bloody, matted hair on the top and side of Longarm's skull. "You got your head cracked open maybe," he said.

"That's what I figured," Longarm muttered. "It wouldn't be the first time."

"First thing is to get you warm," Wells said. "I'll build a fire."

"Thanks."

"Thing is, I got some fellers on my tail. If they see the fire and come to investigate, I'll have to light out. You understand?"

"Build the fire," Longarm muttered. "There's matches in my saddlebag."

When the flames were leaping high, giving off considerable warmth, Wells dragged Longarm closer to the fire, then covered him with his slicker, after which he sat down cross-legged in front of Longarm and regarded him critically.

"How do you feel now?"

"Better."

"You're still shivering."

"Not as much."

"You're a tough one, you are. Trying to tackle them two drifters all by your lonesome, then riding around with a busted skull."

"This ain't the first time I've been so foolish—or unlucky."

"Well, my advice to you is not to make a habit of it."

"I'll try not to."

"You should've let them two killers go their own way."

"I couldn't do that."

"No. And I guess if I'd been in your shoes, I wouldn't't've been able to do that either." He grinned at Longarm. "Too bad good advice is so hard to follow, ain't it?"

Longarm managed a feeble smile in turn. "It is that."

"Looks like this's been an unlucky night for both of us. I'm done in and I guess you are too. What we both need now is a drink."

"There's a bottle of Maryland rye in my saddlebag," Longarm told him. "I don't know how much is left, though."

Wells got eagerly to his feet, found the bottle, and sloshed it. "There's plenty," he said.

He unstoppered the bottle and gulped down a couple of hefty belts, then handed the bottle to Longarm. Earlier, unwilling to add intoxication to his other ills, Longarm had not pulled out the bottle even when his canteen had gone dry. Now, however, he took the bottle willingly, and the two men passed it back and forth until it was drained. By that time the campfire had died to a few glowing embers.

"How you feeling now?" Wells asked.

"Better."

The chattering of Longarm's teeth had subsided noticeably, and he was no longer shivering. The slicker, the fire—and then the Maryland rye had worked wonders.

Wells stomped out the remaining embers of the campfire, and wrapped the slicker about Longarm's bedroll and tied it back onto the cantle, after which he helped Longarm get back onto his feet and guided him over to the chestnut.

"I'll get you as close to Iron City as I can," Wells told Longarm as he boosted him up into his saddle. "But I can't promise anything for sure. This here is an uncertain world." He grinned up at Longarm. "But I guess you already know that."

Longarm said nothing, concentrating instead on gathering up the reins. The exertion expended getting to the horse had set his head to rocking again, and in order to remain in the saddle, he had to reach out and grab the saddlehorn. His mouth suddenly dry once more, he asked Wells for some water from the canteen.

Wells lifted the canteen off the saddlehorn, unscrewed it, and handed it up to him. As Longarm grabbed it, Wells

11

suddenly held up a finger to alert Longarm.

"Listen."

At first Longarm could hear nothing, then came the distant thunder of galloping horses coming from the east. Soon the sound filled the night. The riders were pushing their mounts, and peering beyond the moonlit stream, Longarm made out a dozen or more horsemen charging across the distant flats, strung out in a long line. It took a surprisingly long time for them to pass out of sight. The staccato beat of pounding hooves faded slowly.

When the night was silent again, Wells took back the canteen and shrugged fatalistically. "I got a mite careless in that Mormon town back there and let a goddamn ace fall out of my sleeve," he explained. "But not before I filled my share of inside straights and emptied more than a few wallets. Them horsemen were the sore losers."

"You been on foot all this time?"

"No. Just more bad luck. The horse I borrowed pulled up lame out on that flat, about the time I spied you heading into these cottonwoods. It didn't look like such a long walk, but I sure as hell blistered my feet gettin' here."

Longarm was too far gone by this time to say much. He concentrated instead on staying in the saddle. Wells left him then and went poking about in the grass. A moment later he handed up to Longarm his .44, then gave him the derringer. Longarm managed to holster the Colt, but almost dropped the derringer.

"That's sure a nice cheater you got here," Wells said, reaching up and clipping the derringer's tiny butt to the chain for Longarm, then dropping it into his fob pocket. "There's times I could've used something like that. Of course, that means I'd have to wear a buttoned vest and

12

a frock coat. Don't know if I could manage that."

With a nod, indicating he was ready to go, Longarm straightened in the saddle. Without further comment, Wells took the chestnut's reins and led it out of the cottonwoods, then splashed across the shallow stream, heading northwest toward Iron City—the same direction those hard-charging riders had taken.

Chapter 2

As he rode on through that hellish night, he grunted involuntarily with every jolt of the chestnut's hooves striking the ground. Each separate individual contact the hooves made with the iron-hard surface caused a sharp explosion deep inside his head. Periodic waves of blackness washed over him, and twice he toppled from his saddle, to be caught each time by Jim Wells, who was finally forced to rope him to the saddlehorn.

He lost track of time, but not long before dawn, it seemed to Longarm, they came in sight of a rancher's cabin on a ridge ahead of them, the small structure flanked by cottonwoods. They were still some distance from Iron City, and Longarm realized that in his present condition, he would never make it. He was grateful when Jim Wells turned the chestnut and led it toward the ridge and the ranch house beyond. The log house was dark, and for a moment Longarm was afraid the place had been abandoned, but as he neared it, he smelled the strong odor of fresh horse manure and could hear the

15

restless stamping of the stock inside the barn. It was still a working ranch, all right.

Outside the barn, Jim Wells halted the chestnut, untied Longarm's hands from the saddlehorn, then pulled him out of the saddle and helped him over to a corral post. Longarm slumped gratefully down on the ground and leaned back against the post, his head spinning sickeningly, the deep-seated pain rocketing wildly as a result of his exertions.

"This is the best I can do for you," Jim Wells told him. "And I'm still goin' to have to take your horse."

"You're welcome to it—and anything else I own."

"That's decent of you, Long. When you get to Iron City, check out the town livery stable. If I get that far, I'll leave the chestnut there for you."

Jim Wells mounted up, tossed Longarm his bedroll and saddlebags, then fired two quick shots into the air to arouse the rancher. As he galloped off into the night, a lantern inside the ranch house flared to life and Longarm heard a woman's voice. A second later a door was flung open and a woman ran out of the ranch horse toward him, a white-haired man with a rifle in his hand at her heels.

And that was all Longarm remembered about that night.

In the days that followed, Longarm came awake occasionally to find himself looking up at the woman he had seen rushing from the ranch house as she bent urgently over him, her face drawn with concern. Another time he came awake in bright sunlight, the wind billowing the curtains at the window, and saw a white-haired man with weary, red-rimmed eyes sitting beside his bed, watching

16

him intently. During that brief moment of lucidity, he became aware of the rope around his wrists and ankles, and realized they had been forced to tie him down.

Brief glimpses of these two came and went throughout the delirium that followed, and whenever his senses cleared enough to attempt it, he tried to thank them for their care and concern, but each time, before he could manage more than a word or two, he sank back into his fevered, disordered state. Finally, on a bright afternoon he awoke suddenly—drenched with sweat, parched, and as hungry as a bear in springtime.

He turned his head to face the window, and saw the familiar lace curtains filling out with a cooling breeze. From outside came the sharp, clear sound of a smithy's hammer ringing on steel. It was that sound that had aroused him. Pushing himself up onto his elbows, he looked beyond the billowing curtains at two large cottonwoods and beyond them, at the sharp outline of young mountains vaulting steeply into the heavens.

He flung aside the blankets covering him, and found he was reclining on sheets that were still soaked from perspiration. He felt light-headed, but with a blessed sense of well-being, as if he had this instant been reborn. The fierce thirst and hunger comforted him; it told him how alive he was. But as he inspected himself more closely, he was alarmed at what he found. His long delirium had turned him into a gaunt joke of his former self. His arms were flabby, bloodless, his hands like fleshless claws. He felt his face. It had been shaved, but not expertly, and there was at least a three days' growth of beard covering it. His mustache had grown too long and ragged and desperately needed trimming. And his hair, reaching

17

almost to his shoulders, was shaggy and unkempt.

Hell's fire, he asked himself, *how long have I been laid up anyway?*

He swung his legs off the bed, grapped the bedpost at the foot of the bed for support, and hauled himself upright. He stood for a moment, swaying uncertainly, then sat back down.

Seldom in his life had he felt this weak. Again he pulled himself erect, and this time managed to stay on his feet. He snatched the blanket off his bed and wrapped it, togalike, around his tall, gaunt form. Then, shuffling carefully along like an invalid, he moved across the floor to the bedroom door and pulled it open.

A woman was busy at a huge black wood stove, her back to him. He recognized her as the woman who had peered so often down at him during these past days and nights. He watched her deft movements—and at once envied her strength and robust health. He pulled the door open wider and cleared his throat.

She spun about to face him.

"Oh, my!" she cried. "You're awake!"

"Awake and on my feet, but just barely," he told her ruefully, his voice sounding scratchy and unreal to him. He tried a smile.

She returned it. She was a very pretty woman with thick auburn hair, wide, lovely brown eyes, and a chin solid and well formed. Closely wrapped in her apron and long pale dress, her breasts swelled opulently above her tiny waist.

"You should get back in bed," she told him. "I mean . . . you should be very weak. Last night you were on fire with fever."

18

"The fever broke," he told her. "And the trouble is, now that I got this far, I don't think I'll be able to make it back to my bed—at least not without some help."

He started to turn about in the doorway then, but lost his balance momentarily.

"Oh, let me," she cried, rushing to his side.

"I think maybe I better, at that."

He dropped one arm about her shoulders and let her help him back to the bed. As he fell back on it, she pulled the blanket off his nakedness and threw it over him, pulling it snugly up to his neck, as calmly and efficiently as if this had become for her a long-standing habit.

She inspected his sheets then, and when she saw how damp they were, she hurried from the room for fresh ones. She remade his bed expertly, rolling him over while she did one side, then repeating the process when she made the other side. He watched her silently, catching the nervous but pleased smiles she occasionally threw his way as she worked.

At last, once she was certain he was secure in a warm bed again, she propped his head up onto a couple of down pillows and stepped back to smile down at her handiwork.

"How's that?" she asked.

"Couldn't be better," he said. "Thanks."

"You are most welcome."

"I guess you're wondering who I am."

She looked suddenly embarrassed. "I am afraid not," she told him. "I . . . well, when I took off your things, your wallet fell out. I looked and saw the badge. So I know who you are. You're Custis Long, a U.S. deputy marshal."

"Guilty, as charged." He smiled. "But don't worry

about looking at the badge and wallet. No harm done."

"My name's Ruth Osborne. I live alone here with my father, Ben."

"I'm much obliged, Ruth—to both of you. Now could I trouble you for a glass of water? I'm as dry as a rain barrel in August."

"Oh, of course."

She hurried from the room to return almost immediately with a glass and pitcher of water. Filling the glass, she handed it to him. He took it from her, emptied it greedily, then handed it back.

"More," he said, grinning.

She refilled the glass. He downed this second one, then sagged back onto his pillow, his thirst slaked.

"You must be hungry too," she commented, smiling.

"I'm as empty as a hollowed-out log," he admitted. "Did I see you preparing supper at that stove?"

"You did. But you won't have to wait that long. I've put aside some broth for you. All I have to do is heat it up."

"Sounds good to me."

She hurried from the room.

But when she returned with the steaming bowl of broth, she found Longarm sleeping peacefully. The broth would have to wait a little longer. But that didn't matter. All that mattered was that this gaunt giant of a man would recover from his grievous head injuries after all.

She tiptoed out of the room, silently closing the door behind her.

A few days later, feeling and looking much stronger, Longarm emerged from the barn and started across the yard to the ranch house, a buzzing halo of horseflies keeping pace with him. He had spent the afternoon cleaning out the stalls and repairing a hole in the barn's roof, and he stank of horse manure and horse piss. Pulling open the kitchen door, he poked his head in. Ruth was standing over the sink, peeling potatoes.

"How about filling a washtub for me?" he suggested. "My nose tells me I need a bath."

She smiled. "I can smell you from here. Go out back in the wash shed. I've already got some water boiling on the stove."

He grinned back at her. "Much obliged."

Longarm went back around to the wash shed and undressed. Ruth's father had taken the flatbed into Iron City that morning to pick up supplies, and Longarm had taken it upon himself to take care of the irksome chores that Ben had been muttering about the day before. In this way he hoped to thank Ben and his daughter for their hospitality—and more. He would not be their guest much longer, and was grateful for any chance to help them before he rode out.

Ruth appeared with two buckets of steaming water. She set them down and took his clothes off the back of the chair where he had left them.

"There's more water coming," she assured him as she left the shed.

Longarm emptied the two buckets of water into the porcelain tub, waited for two more that Ruth brought, and emptied them in also. As she went after more, he stepped gingerly into the tub, waited for the stinging to subside, then gently lowered himself into the steaming water. He was just getting adjusted to it when Ruth appeared with

21

a bucket of cold water. Before he could stop her, she poured the icy water over his head and shoulders. He was too startled to cry out, and with an impish grin, she pushed his head under the water. He surfaced, blowing like a seal, and reached out to grab her, but she danced lightly back, still laughing.

Then she grabbed a big yellow cake of lye soap, lathered thoroughly a stiff-bristled brush, and proceeded to scrub his back and shoulders, working efficiently, leaning over him as she scrubbed, showing neither a raised eyebrow nor a blush at sight of his nakedness. Indeed, throughout his convalescence, her reaction to his manhood had been closer to that of a sister regarding her brother than that of a mature woman to a healthy male.

When she finished scrubbing him, she dipped a saucepan into the water and rinsed him off thoroughly.

"There," she said, putting the saucepan down and brushing a lock of damp hair off her forehead. "I must say, you've got a lot of back there, Custis."

"Is there any skin left on it?"

"Oh, my, you poor dear. Did I scrub too hard?"

"I'm not worried. When new skin grows back, I'll be as good as new."

"Stop complaining!"

He chuckled. "Thanks, Ruth. No kidding. There are some places a man can't reach easy, and you sure enough cleaned them spots real good. I feel about ten pounds lighter."

Ruth was looking into his eyes now, and in that instant Longarm knew she was no longer seeing the helpless, delirious invalid who had lain for so long in her bed, but

22

the man these past few days had made him—a healthy male animal whose piercing gaze, thick shock of brown hair, and angular, lean face were arousing in her something a lot more urgent than sisterly concern.

He stepped out of the tub, fully aroused, and took the towel off the back of the chair where she had laid it. Draping it over his shoulder, he stood calmly before her. In some confusion she glanced down at him.

"Oh," she cried, taking a step back.

He stepped closer and pulled her gently against him. She started to struggle, but stopped as his lips closed about hers. Swiftly her arms snaked about his neck as she clung to him fiercely, her lips working frantically, her passionate need almost outstripping his.

Panting, she pushed away, then took his hand and led him into the ranch house. He knew her intent as they approached the bedroom, and held back.

"What about your father?" he asked. "He should be coming back soon."

"He won't be back until late."

"You sure? Iron City's not all that far."

"Pa likes to wet his whistle at the Last Chance Saloon, and when he gets back, he'll be singing his fool head off. We'll have to lift him down from the wagon and put him to bed. Now get in here, dammit!"

Longarm argued no more and let Ruth pull him into the bedroom. She lifted off her dress and flung it aside. To his pleased surprise, he found she had prepared for this moment and was wearing nothing under the dress. She opened her arms to him. It had been a long, long time for both of them. He stepped into her open arms, impaling her gently as he bent her backward onto the

23

bed. She gasped with pleasure, their lack of foreplay no problem; she was already dripping wet, her muff hot, pulsing, devouring him eagerly.

Dusk was falling when, a good while later, Longarm rolled off her and came to rest at her side, panting slightly, a delicious drowsiness stealing over him.

Ruth propped herself up on an elbow. "Are you surprised?"

"At you?"

"At my . . . hunger."

"Nope. You said you were married. I reckon it's been a long time for you, just as it has for me."

"Sometimes, in my need for him, I'd think I could welcome him back. But then I'd get my senses and keep myself busy. He was a mean-spirited rattlesnake. After him, I swore I'd never marry again. And I won't. But that don't mean you and I couldn't make a go of it here. This ranch could really grow into something if it had a real man running it."

"I'm a lawman, Ruth. I like it. I don't think I'm fit to stay in one place for long."

She sighed. "Well, just thought I'd let you know you were welcome."

"I appreciate the offer." Then he grinned at her. "I'm starvin'. What you got for supper?"

"It'll be a late supper," she said.

"I could eat a side of beef."

"Will a leg of lamb do?"

"Nicely."

She sat up quickly. "Lay still. Take a nap if you want, while I prepare it."

He watched her pluck her dress off the back of the chair and drop it down over her head, then sit down before her dressing table to comb out her long auburn hair. Soon, she had it reaching clear down her back in a single, gleaming curl. As the brush flashed, he heard her begin to hum softly to herself, and watching her, Longarm felt proud to think he might have had something to do with the way she felt now. Too bad there was no way he could take her up on that invitation.

But he still had those two killers to find so they could lead him to that gang tearing up this territory. They were somewhere in those mountains looming on the horizon, deep in among their gaunt, twisting canyons and the treeless alkaline flats beyond. He had spent time in Utah on other assignments and knew those mountains well. If ever the devil had taken a hand in shaping a land, this place was it—a baked dry, hellish landscape cruel enough to attract only the meanest and wildest of outcasts.

Iron City was in an uproar.

As Ruth pulled the team to a halt in front of the livery, a crowd of townsmen surged by them to halt in front of the Wells Fargo Express office, where a moment before, as she and Longarm rode in, a dust-coated stage had pulled up. The Express office was diagonally across the street from the livery, and as the excited townsfolk milled around the stage, some of them passed close beside the flatbed.

"What's happened?" Ruth asked one of the men.

"The stage was held up!" the man told her excitedly.

"Was anyone hurt?"

"Danny Winthrop was shot dead, and old Sam Keys is hurt bad."

"My God," Ruth cried, turning to Longarm in dismay. "I knew Winthrop. He has a wife and a boy not much older than ten."

"You know Winthrop's missus?"

"Yes. Oh, Custis, this is terrible."

"This sort of thing's gettin' to be a habit around here, huh?"

"Honestly, Longarm, this is almost too much. That gang seems to be able to rob stages at will, and there's nothing anyone can do to stop them."

"Sounds bad," Longarm agreed, slinging his saddle-bags over his shoulder and reaching back for his bedroll. He was packing his .44-40 in his cross-draw rig under his brown tweed frock coat; the gold chain was draped across his vest, his mean little derringer resting in the watch-fob pocket. Any rips or other wear his suit and shirt had suffered Ruth had mended with great care and skill while he was at the ranch. Now, his suit freshly pressed, the tips of his longhorn mustache flaring defiantly, he felt almost as good as new.

"Do me a favor," he said to Ruth as he hopped down off the seat. "Don't tell anyone in town who I am—if anyone asks, that is. I'm just a hard-luck drifter you nursed back to health."

"All right, Longarm. My lips are sealed."

"I'll go in and see about my chestnut. And maybe you can go find Winthrop's widow and give her some comfort."

"Yes," Ruth agreed somberly, "I'll go do that."

Custis reached up and took Ruth's hand. "Thanks, Ruth. Thanks to you and your pa—for everything."

She smiled warmly down at him. "You've already thanked us enough, Custis. I'll miss you. Pa will too. I hope you find those men—so maybe then you could come back. For a visit anyway."

"That's a promise."

Custis stepped back, watched her for a moment as she drove on through the crowd, then strode into the livery stable. There was no hostler about; he was probably a part of that crowd in front of the Express office. Longarm pushed on into the stable and came upon the chestnut in a rear stall. Not really surprised that Jim Wells had done as he had promised, he reached out for the chestnut and stroked its head. It looked sleek and healthy, if maybe a little restless from being cooped up in this stall so long.

Longarm stepped back as he heard someone entering the livery.

"Hey, there, mister," the hostler cried, "what're you doin' messin' with that horse?"

Longarm turned to face the hostler. He was a thin, rheumy-eyed man pushing sixty with long chin-whiskers and a decided limp. He had snatched up a pitchfork upon entering and was hefting it menacingly as he approached.

"This here's my chestnut," Longarm explained. "A friend of mine left it here for me."

"A friend of yours, you say. And who might that be?"

"Jim Wells."

The hostler nodded. "He said you'd be in for the horse. Didn't say it would take this long for you to get here, though."

"I came as fast as I could."

"I got your saddle and Winchester in my room back there. You can take them anytime you want. My name's Hoss. Leastways that's what everyone calls a stove-up cowpoke when he takes a job in a town livery."

"I've noticed."

Hoss rubbed the white stubble on his gaunt cheek. "Well, now," he said, studying the chestnut. "This here animal warn't no trouble, but he sure knew what to do with a bagful of grain." He looked shrewdly at Longarm. "How'd ten dollars be?"

"Fair enough."

Longarm paid the man, then asked if he knew where he might find Jim Wells.

"He's gone, mister. And there's some who'd say good riddance. It wasn't so bad, him using marked cards. But he should've kept his tool to home, if you know what I mean. He got real friendly with the barber's wife and left town in a hurry, his naked backside peppered with buckshot."

Longarm shook his head. It sounded like Jim Wells, all right. Longarm asked for directions to the town's best hotel.

"The hotel's a couple of blocks further down, the other side of the street."

"I said the best hotel."

"Mister, it has to be the best. It's the only one we got."

Longarm left the livery. In order to cross to the other side, he was forced to push through the crowd still clustered around the bullet-riddled stagecoach. He was halfway through it when the sheriff, a couple of deputies by his side, stepped out onto the Express office's loading platform and began to address the crowd.

Longarm halted to listen.

" . . . Danny and Sam are dead!"

An angry mutter swept the crowd. Someone shouted a question at the sheriff, demanding what he planned to do.

"I'm going after them!" the sheriff replied. "I say it's time for us to stop this here gang's killin' and robbin'. I'm forming a posse right now and I want volunteers."

But instead of the enthusiastic response Longarm had expected from the crowd, the men shifted uneasily and began muttering under their breath, obviously more than reluctant to join in any posse. Some of the townsmen started to slip away.

"Hell, Sheriff," a blacksmith standing in front of Longarm shouted, "them road agents'd be long gone by now. It'd be the same thing all over again! We'll never find 'em. It'd just be a waste of good horseflesh."

"Mel's right, Sheriff," another man standing behind Longarm cried out. "We're gettin' sick of beatin' our tails off and coming back with nothing but alkali dust."

"That's the truth," another townsman called out. "Them bastards're probably back in their hole by now. We might as well try rope smoke."

"We'd just be chasin' shadows all over again!"

"The only thing we'll catch is sore bottoms!"

"You're wrong!" the sheriff insisted. "All of you. This time it'll be different. This time we'll get them. And its time for you citizens to do something beside belly-ache."

29

The townsmen that were still near the platform moved restlessly, arguing unhappily among themselves, discussing what they should do, obviously stung by the sheriff's taunts. But it was clear to Longarm that there was not a man there who was eager to follow this sheriff in pursuit of the gang that had just robbed the stagecoach.

One of the men, a skinny gent with red hair, strode closer to the Express platform. "Sheriff," he said, "you got any idea where they might be holin' up?"

"Skull Canyon."

This statement caught every man's attention—including Longarm. He found himself moving on through the crowd toward the Express platform.

"What makes you say that, Blowser?" the redhead asked.

"Look, Tex, ain't that where you'd go if you was runnin' from the law?"

"Ain't had no experience running from the law," Tex replied.

A little man in a huge sombrero stepped up beside the redhead. "I remember the last time, Sheriff. You was certain sure the gang was holed up at Sundown Creek."

"This here's the Skull Canyon Gang," the sheriff insisted.

Longarm and the rest of the townsmen moved closer, every man studying the sheriff intently.

"How do you know that for sure?" Tex persisted.

"I didn't want to mention it, but before Sam died, he said he recognized one of the highwaymen. He said it was Charlie Biddle. That spells Skull Canyon to me."

"I heard the gang all wore masks," Tex said. "How could Sam recognize him?"

"Look, Tex, if Sam says he recognized him, that's enough for me."

"You know where that canyon is, Sheriff?"

"Sure, I do."

"Then *you* ride in there and get your ass blown off."

Tex turned away and with a few of his buddies clustered about him strode off down the street, heading for the nearest saloon. At once others in the crowd began to move off as well. A few nervous, bonneted women hurried over to pull away most of the remaining townsmen, leaving only four townsmen to join the sheriff and his two deputies in this posse.

Longarm didn't hesitate as he stepped up onto the platform alongside the four townsmen. He had just stumbled on what he perceived to be the perfect way for him to track the Skull Canyon Gang. Still, a prudent caution told him not to reveal his identity to the sheriff. There was no need to crowd the man by revealing his rank as a federal officer.

"Count me in, Sheriff," Longarm told him.

"Who're you? I ain't seen you around here before."

"I just rode in."

"You're a stranger? How come you're so anxious to ride with me?"

"I'm a law-abidin' citizen, Sheriff. You asked for men to join your posse to help bring in these highwaymen, didn't you? You got so many volunteers you can afford to turn me down?"

"What's your name?"

"Custis Long."

"Where you from?"

"I been stayin' at the Osborne ranch."

The sheriff's eyes narrowed. "Yeah, I heard about you. Ruth's old man said you was out of your head when they found you. You sure you ain't still a mite loose in the head?"

"My head's all fixed, Sheriff. Don't worry about me."

"We'll be ridin' a long ways," the sheriff warned.

"Look, Sheriff, do you want to form a posse and get after that gang—or would you rather stand here and argue with me? I thought you wanted volunteers to help you track these outlaws."

The sheriff took a deep breath and nodded. "You made your point, Long. If you think you can handle it, come ahead."

"I'll get my horse and the rest of my gear, Sheriff."

"We'll meet in front of my office," the sheriff told him. "I'll swear in you and these other four men. We'll be ridin' out soon after that. Make sure you got enough provisions to last a while—a week, at least."

Not long after, a deputy's star pinned to his vest, Longarm rode out with Sheriff Blowser's posse, wondering as he rode why the sheriff had appeared so lacking in enthusiasm at the prospect of Longarm riding with him.

Chapter 3

In the days that followed, Longarm took the opportunity to study closely the sheriff and his fellow posse members.

The sheriff's name was Gil Blowser. He was a big, florid gent with a drooping mustache stained yellow from tobacco juice. His small, buttonlike eyes were set close together. He spat a lot, talked with a quiet menace—and seemed to know the country well. He carried a well-oiled Smith and Wesson in his leather holster, and like most lawmen hired to hold these young Western towns together, Longarm guessed Blowser might once have worked the other side of the law, his election to the sheriff's office an illustration of the adage that it took a rat to fight a rat.

Longarm wondered which side this rat was on today.

The strangest and most flamboyant of the posse's four volunteers was Tim O'Malley. He wore a black patch over his left eye, and had little hair on his head and a constant expression sour enough to curdle milk at ten paces.

He wore a black floppy-brimmed hat and kept a dusty cloak thrown over his shoulders that filled out behind him as he rode. He spoke only when spoken to, and then in a harsh, cutting tone laced with scathing derision. His Navy Colt sat in a well-oiled holster he kept tied down with a rawhide thong. In his warbag he carried a bible, the pages of which he tore out to use for building cigarettes, which dangled constantly from his thin, mean lips.

Mike Smithers stuck close by O'Malley, despite O'Malley's seemingly fierce contempt for him. Smithers had shoulder-length white hair and a pink, wrinkled face. Two heavy cartridge belts sagged across his chest, and he wore a battered felt hat with a red feather stuck in the hat band. His only weapon was an ancient Walker Colt, which he was forever cleaning, and a buffalo skinner's knife. He kept his mouth shut despite O'Malley's relentless picking at him, seemingly grateful to be allowed to tag along with him.

Will Coombs was the loner in the bunch. A wild-eyed, sullen misfit, he rode hunched over in his saddle. He wore a black hat and Levi's, with a filthy red-and-gold serape flung permanently over his shoulders. He had no holsters and carried his two Colts stuck in his belt; as he rode he muttered continually to himself. No one understood what he was mumbling about, and no one appeared to give a damn.

Hound was a tall, bony character with a mournful droop to his face and sad, liquid eyes. He resembled an unhappy basset hound, and as he rode he complained unhappily about every mile they put behind them. At the close of the first day's ride, Hound assumed the role of cook, a position he kept from then on. He turned out to be an excellent cook, his eyes lighting up with enthusiasm whenever he had occasion to use his long skinning knife on the fresh meat Longarm and the other posse members occasionally bagged for him. His son-of-a-bitch stew was the best Longarm had ever tasted.

The sheriff's two deputies, Chet Breed and Burrel Wilson, kept close to the sheriff at all times. Breed was a dirty, unkempt fellow with a yellow grin who seemed content to snicker sidelong at the cracks of his companions, providing them with a constantly appreciative, sniggering audience. His companion, Wilson, was one of those men who seemed incapable of doing anything smoothly or quietly—from unsaddling his horse to pouring a cup of coffee. He spoke in a loud, unpleasant voice, his observations punctuated by a raw bark most of the time. It was a relief to Longarm that he spoke primarily to his buddy, Breed.

To Longarm the posse members were civil enough, yet they seemed to share a secret, hidden understanding, giving Longarm the impression he'd joined a party already in progress. It became more and more obvious to him that all of the posse members—including the sheriff and his two deputies—were old acquaintances. They enjoyed private jokes and reminiscences without making any attempt to bring Longarm into it; and while in Longarm's presence, they kept close-mouthed and taciturn. It was as if, by joining this posse, Longarm had intruded on an old family reunion. A very old and secretive family.

But was it really a posse?

Longarm had been watching the curiously lackluster pace the sheriff and his posse were taking as they tracked the highwaymen who had robbed the stage. There seemed to be no sense of urgency at all. Recalling the complaints of the townsmen back in Iron City, Longarm saw now how accurate they'd been. At this rate, the only thing this posse was likely to catch was a cold—from the drop of temperature they had to endure when night fell.

Longarm decided he would challenge the sheriff the first chance he got.

It came on the fourth day out when Blowser paused in front of Longarm to peer about him at the rocky landscape. It was near dusk, and he wasn't looking for tracks, but for a place to set down his bedroll.

"Sheriff," Longarm said, "we been limpin' after this gang for four days now. Maybe if we rode a mite faster, we'd catch up to them."

Longarm was reclining on the ground, his back resting against a boulder still warm from the day's wicked sun. The sheriff turned his head to look down at Longarm.

"That what you think, Long?"

"Just a thought, Sheriff."

"Nice to have your opinion, Long. But don't you worry none. You'll be meeting up with highwaymen soon enough."

"Glad you think so, Sheriff."

"Take my word for it."

"Just so it's before the first winter snows."

The sheriff was being very patient with Longarm. Now his eyebrows shot up a notch at Longarm's sarcasm. "Maybe you ain't satisfied with the way I'm runnin' this posse?"

"Maybe I'm not, at that."

"Now, just what's eatin' at you, Long?"

"Well, for one thing, I been noticing that ever since we set out, we've been taking no precautions."

"Precautions? What're you talkin' about?"

"At night, we make no effort to hide our campfires."

"You think that's important, do you?"

"And we ain't been sending out any scouts to look for sign."

"Anything else?"

"Like I said before, at the pace we're taking, we won't catch up with anything—except maybe winter."

"You want us to run these horses into the ground?"

"No, and I don't want moss coverin' them either. This ain't no posse, Blowser. It's a Sunday school picnic, eight riders strong."

"That what you think?" the sheriff responded with surprising mildness.

"That's the way I see it."

"Well, now," Blowser continued soothingly, "you're sure enough entitled to your opinion. Just don't go getting your bowels in an uproar. Maybe you'll find out soon enough which one of us is full of shit. Get some sleep now. We'll get a fresh start in the morning."

The other posse members had heard the exchange and had remained perfectly still as they stood around the campfire so they would not miss a word. Now, as the sheriff joined them, they talked quietly together, and soon they were yelping and howling with poorly suppressed laughter.

The sound of this yokel laughter did not comfort Longarm, and he slept fitfully that night, his finger tucked about his .44's trigger.

• • •

Late the next day, Blowser was riding a few lengths ahead of the posse when he rounded a huge, flanking wall of rock and pulled up suddenly.

"There it is," he cried to the rest of the posse, pointing.

Longarm rode up to him with the others and pulled his chestnut to a halt. The sheriff was pointing at the entrance to a canyon. Skull Canyon. It was aptly named. The canyon's right flank—a slab of white, pebbly rock—gazed down at the posse members, its ridges and hollows resembling with uncanny fidelity a sun-bleached skull right down to the dark, hollow sockets.

"That's where the bastards are holed up," the sheriff said to Longarm. "You mark my words."

Then he addressed the other members of the posse. "We'll camp out here and wait until daybreak. Then we'll move in on them—catch the sons of bitches with their pants down."

"You know that canyon, Sheriff?" Longarm asked.

"I know this country."

"Looks like a pretty big canyon."

"It is—once you get inside."

"So what makes you think we'll find the highwaymen once we get inside?"

"What makes you think we won't?"

"I told you. It looks like a pretty big canyon."

"There's a cabin in there. I know where it is. I'm thinkin' that's where they've holed up."

"I hope you're right, Sheriff."

"We all do, Long," said O'Malley, speaking directly to Longarm for the first time in two days. "Why don't you let the sheriff run this show and keep your mouth shut?"

His words were uttered with such contempt that Longarm was momentarily startled. As he cleared his throat to respond, O'Malley nudged his horse alongside Longarm's and leaned closer, his single eye studying Longarm the way a cat would a mouse he had not yet snapped up.

"The sheriff knows what he's about," O'Malley said. "If he says there's a cabin in there, well, then, that's where it is. And that's where them outlaws are."

"You know this cabin, do you?"

"Sure he does," said Mike Smithers, working his horse closer. "O'Malley and me, we stayed in it one time."

"Where is it?"

"Near a stream. About a mile up the canyon."

"Shut up," Blowser told Smithers. "No sense in all this palaver. I say we give ourselves and our horses a rest before we go in there to tackle them highwaymen. They're sure to be well armed and rested up by now."

Tim O'Malley straightened in his saddle as did his partner, Smithers, both riders regarding Longarm now with a kind of amused contempt—as if they knew a secret Longarm would give a lot to know.

Blowser grinned suddenly at Longarm. "You think you'll be ready to go in there with us, Long?"

"I'll be ready."

They found a campsite in a pine grove nearby. As Longarm dismounted and unsaddled his horse, he could feel the eyes of the posse members watching him. It gave him an itchy feeling between his shoulder blades, and he found himself wondering what this posse was really up to. He had no doubt that was Skull Canyon he had just seen, and there might well be a cabin in there somewhere just as Sheriff Blowser insisted—but as sure as little boys eat green apples, they were not going to find a desperate band of highwaymen holed up inside it.

And maybe the members of the gang Longarm had been searching for were right here in this pine grove, their cold eyes drilling a hole in his back. It was a wild thought, and not a very pleasant one. But he didn't see how he could discount it altogether.

An hour or so before sunup, they moved into the canyon, Blowser in the lead. He seemed to know where he was going as he led them up a narrow game trail to the canyon's rim. In the cool pre-dawn darkness, they dismounted and tethered their horses in a patch of scrub pine. Longarm, hanging back from the others, dismounted and turned his chestnut back down the trail.

When he caught up to the posse, he moved with them along the rim of the canyon until they came into sight of a small cabin nestled in the bend of a sluggish stream below them. An outhouse and a barn stood beside it, and in the corral alongside the barn stood a single horse. It moved nervously in the new day's freshening light. Longarm moved up beside the sheriff.

"Where's all the horses?" Longarm muttered, checking his Winchester's load as he moved closer to the rim's edge. "Don't look like there's much of a gang down there."

"There inside the barn."

"Yeah," said Will Coombs, his eyes gleaming with a mad light as he peered at Longarm. "Why don't you go down there, Marshal Long, and make sure."

"Shut up!" the sheriff told him.

But the cat was out of the bag. As Longarm had begun to suspect, everyone in this posse had known from the beginning knew who he was—and what he was doing in this territory.

"You know who I am, Sheriff?"

"Yep. Ben Osborne was braggin' about having a deputy U.S. marshal holed up in his place the last time he was in town."

"Well, then, let's go ahead now and see what we've got down there in that cabin."

"You sound like you're taking charge, Long."

"I'm just curious, that's all. I want to see what you and this slow-motion posse are up to."

"We're up to catching outlaws, that's what," said Chet Breed, levering a fresh round into his rifle's firing chamber.

Beside him, Tim O'Malley took his two huge Colts out of his belt and thumb-cocked them. The combined racket the two men made echoed sharply in the still, morning air. Turning away from Longarm, the sheriff peered down at the cabin. There was no light showing from inside. The outlaws—if there were any inside—were still sleeping.

"Well, let's get down there," said Longarm.

"Aw, hell," said the sheriff, with a quick wink at Chet Breed, "there ain't no call for us to go on down there. We can handle them bastards easy enough from up here."

"How in hell do you plan to do that?" Longarm demanded.

"When I give the signal, we'll open up on the cabin. Them walls are as thin as newspaper. Our fire will cut them highwaymen to pieces."

41

"You aren't going to call out, warn those inside?"

"Why bother? We know who's in there. We trailed them all the way, didn't we?"

"You didn't trail a single rider."

"Shut up, Long. This is my posse, not yours."

"You heard him, Marshal," said O'Malley. "When the sheriff gives the signal, we're all goin' to open up on that cabin down there. That means you too."

"Does it?"

Chet Breed and Burt Wilson moved up beside Longarm. "Yep, Marshal," Breed said, exposing his yellow teeth. "That's what it means."

"Shut up, all of you," Blowser said, lifting his rifle up to his shoulder and sighting on the cabin.

Blowser fired. There was a tiny puff of dust where the slug tore through the cabin wall. At once the rest of the posse opened up. There were two windows, one on each side of the door. In less than a minute both windows had been shattered, their sashes broken and hanging in the window frames. For three or four minutes the canyon echoed with the deadly rattle of the fierce, murderous fusillade.

Abruptly the cabin door sagged open, and a lone figure appeared in the doorway, his tall frame leaning crookedly against the doorjamb. He had taken one slug already and Longarm could see the gleam of hot blood high on his shirtfront. He could see something else just as clearly—the man's face.

It was Wells! Jim Wells, the man who had saved his life!

Chapter 4

"Hold your fire!" Longarm shouted at the others. "That's no outlaw! Stop firing!"

Startled, the posse members held up and turned to stare at him.

"What the hell you yellin' for?" demanded the sheriff. "How do you know he ain't?"

"You know who that is. Jim Wells."

"So what?"

"He never robbed a stage in his life—and you know it."

"Aw, shit," said Tim O'Malley. "If you ain't got the stomach for this, shut up and let us be."

The men turned their attention back to the wounded man still in sight below them. Still propped up in the cabin doorway, he was waving a white flag. Ignoring it, the posse resumed firing on him.

Longarm grabbed the barrel of Tim O'Malley's rifle, twisted it out of his hands, flung it into the brush behind them, then, with the barrel of his Winchester, sent Mike

Smithers's rifle spinning into the canyon. Whirling, Hound backed hastily away from Longarm. Longarm went after him, but before he could reach him, the sheriff grabbed his right arm and flung him violently around as Chet Breed and Burrel Wilson fell on him from behind; Longarm spun out of their grasp just as the sheriff fired at him. He missed, and Longarm headed for the protection of a large boulder sitting on the canyon rim.

By this time every member of the posse had turned their fire on him, and as he ducked behind the boulder, a hornet's nest of whining lead ricocheted off its face. Keeping low, he kept on past the boulder and plunged down the steep slope into the canyon, heading for the cabin below. As he scrambled lower, he grabbed at the scrub pine and projecting ledges with his right hand to keep himself from toppling into the canyon. Meanwhile, the posse continued to blast away at him from the canyon rim. With the angry snarl of hot lead still whining past his ears, Longarm ducked finally into a stand of pine. The bullets followed after him, slicing off branches and pine cones, their debris clattering off Longarm's hat brim.

Deeper in the pines, Longarm paused to look back through the branches at the posse above him. They were crouched low, pouring fire down at the cabin, but Longarm could hear return fire now coming from the direction of the cabin.

As he broke from the timber a moment later he saw Jim Wells, crouching behind a corner of the cabin, firing up at the posse with his sixgun. He was using his left hand, and Longarm saw at once the big chunk missing from his right shoulder.

"Keep it up," Longarm called to him. "I need the cover."

"Come ahead!"

There was a creek between Longarm and the cabin. Keeping his ass and his head down, Longarm bolted to the creek, splashed across it, ran up the bank to the cabin, and flung himself down beside Wells.

"Custis Long! It's you!" Wells cried, astonished. "Hey, you mind tellin' me what's going on?"

"I'll explain later," Longarm told him, lifting his rifle and sending a round at O'Malley's floppy-brimmed hat just visible above the ridge. He saw a tiny geyser of dirt just in front of it and the hat vanished from sight.

"Just who *are* those guys?" Wells demanded.

"That's Sheriff Blowser and his posse."

"Blowser? What's he opening up on me for?"

"You just got elected."

"For what?"

Longarm quickly sighted on another posse member running along the rim and squeezed off a shot. He missed, but the posse member ducked away from the canyon ridge. "You're the gang of highwaymen who robbed the stage a few days back."

"Me? Rob a stage?"

"That's right."

"I didn't rob no stage. Blowser must be crazy."

"Yeah. He's as crazy as a fox."

"Dammit, Long, who the hell are you anyway? Every time you show up, there's trouble."

"I'm a U.S. deputy marshal, Jim. And I'm out here after the Skull Canyon Gang."

"That gang that's been raisin' hell around here?"

45

"And that just robbed the stage."

"You got any idea where they are?"

"Sure. They're up there on the ridge, firing down at us. The sheriff's their leader, looks like. He let me ride in here with him to show me how sincere a lawman he was and how eager he was to bring the gang to justice. Only I didn't buy it. He knows now he's got to kill me. And you too, I suppose, since you're a witness."

"Sounds pretty damn complicated to me. What do we do now?"

"Get the hell out of here."

"I'm hit bad. Leave me here. I'll cover you."

"I'm not leaving you."

"Don't be a fool. The slug's still in my shoulder and I've lost plenty of blood. My head's spinnin' so bad I won't be able to stay in a saddle."

"Let me worry about that."

"Then we'll need another horse. Where's yours?"

"Back down the canyon. We'll ride double on your horse, head back down the canyon. There's a chance we'll find the chestnut waiting for me."

The gunfire from the ridge had tailed off by this time. But not completely. Every once in a while a posse member would put a slug in the wall just above their heads or close beside the spot where they were huddled, and by this time not a single windowpane was still intact.

While Wells continued to fire on anyone he saw moving along the canyon rim, Longarm slipped back to the corral, pulled the horse into the barn, and saddled it. When he was ready, he called out to Wells, who ducked around the cabin and into the barn. Longarm helped the man up behind him on the horse. They both checked their Colts, lowered their heads, and charged out of the barn and down the canyon. A sudden fusillade opened up on them from the slope farther down, and Longarm realized that the sheriff had planned to rush the canyon. Ducking low, they charged on past the posse members, and a quarter of a mile farther on, not far from the canyon entrance, Longarm caught sight of the chestnut cropping the grass behind a clump of cottonwoods.

Pulling to a halt beside it, Longarm handed the reins to Wells, dropped to the ground, then mounted the chestnut. From behind them they could hear the pounding of hooves as the posse, mounted now, came after them.

Longarm looked around at Wells. "You think you can ride a few more miles?"

"Hell, yes," he responded gamely. "Just keep an eye on me. I might fall off."

He didn't fall off, but he was soon riding raggedly, and Longarm slowed up to keep pace with him. Wells's face was ashen and drawn with the pain of his wound, but somehow he kept on the horse. About a mile beyond the canyon, a dim flurry of gunfire came from behind them. Longarm glanced back and saw that the sheriff and his posse were gaining on them swiftly. Reaching over, Longarm snatched up the reins of Wells's horse and urged both horses to a full gallop. Wells, slumped over the saddlehorn, hung on grimly.

They were deep into the mountains by this time. Longarm crossed a long, hard-baked alkali flat and plunged into a tortuous, twisting canyon, then followed a series of arroyos, one folding back upon the other, until he broke out onto a canyon. Halfway down it, he spied a cave hidden by a clump of stunted pines about fifty yards above the canyon floor. Longarm would not have seen it had he not glanced back when he had to see how close behind him his pursuers were.

Fortunately, they were still well out of sight. Longarm dismounted and pulled Wells from his saddle, and left the man leaning against a boulder while he led both horses back up the canyon until he found a narrow draw where he could tether them. He returned to Wells with their gear, cached it under some bushes, then slung the nearly unconscious man over his shoulder and lugged him up the steep slope to the cave. He set Wells down gently and climbed back down to the floor of the canyon, found a mesquite bush, cut off some of its branches, then brushed them along the trail, wiping out their tracks for a good three hundred yards back, breaking off at a dry wash heading in a southerly direction he just might have taken.

He returned to the cave with their gear, peeled off Wells's blood-heavy shirt, and took a look at the man's wound. Wells was mistaken. The slug was not still in his shoulder. It had gone all the way through; but it had torn up a lot of muscle and flesh as it did so, and Wells had lost a considerable amount of blood. Worse, the ragged wound was already festering. The bleeding would have to be stanched, the wound cauterized.

"Good news," he told Wells.

"What's that?"

"The bullet went on through."

"That's not the way it feels."

"That's the way it is. You got any whiskey in your saddlebags?"

"I had some. But it's been a lonely, thirsty time out here, and I'm fresh out."

"Too bad. Means I'll have to cauterize the wound with something else."

"Ouch."

"Sorry."

"That bad, is it?"

"Before long, you'll be able to smell it."

"Do what you have to. I'm too weak to protest."

Longarm was considering whether or not to build a fire to heat his knife when he heard the sound of shod hooves striking stone below them in the canyon. Both men froze. Longarm moved to the mouth of the cave and peered down through the pines. He saw nothing for a moment or two—then watched as Sheriff Blowser and the others rode into view.

The sheriff was not keeping his eyes to the ground, which meant he wasn't following any tracks, just scouting, hoping to pick up their trail again. The posse passed underneath the cave and disappeared on up the canyon. Longarm watched until they were well out of sight, then pulled back into the cave and returned to Wells.

"What do you think?" Wells asked.

"They've lost our trail. Looks like they're just searchin' through the badlands, hoping to pick it up again. They'll get sick of it before long and head back to Iron City."

"We hope."

"But I don't want to build a fire. Not yet. I got another idea."

"What is it?"

"Thing is, it'll hurt like hell."

"Don't tell me any more. Just go ahead and do it."

Longarm rummaged in Wells's bedroll and found a clean white shirt. He promptly tore it into strips. With each sound of the tearing cloth, Wells winced.

"That was my best shirt," Wells sighed.

When Longarm finished tearing the shirt into strips, he inspected the wound once more, then unholstered his Colt, and humming softly to distract Wells, slipped around behind him and with a swift, downward chop clipped him on the back of his head. Uttering a barely audible sigh, Wells settled sideways to the floor of the cave, unconscious.

Working swiftly, Longarm emptied the gunpowder from six shells into the wound, struck a match, and dropped it onto the gunpowder. There was a soft, searing flare, then a smudgy smoke that smelled faintly of burning flesh. Waving the smoke away, Longarm peered into the wound. He saw blackened, singed flesh, but no pus. Even as he watched, fresh, bright blood began to well out past the puckered flesh. Quickly, he bound the wound as tightly as he could to stanch the flow of blood. That done, he leaned Wells back against the wall of the cave and waited.

After a few minutes, Wells opened his eyes and stared groggily at Longarm.

"What happened? It felt like the roof of this cave came down on me."

"Not the cave, my Colt."

"Jesus."

"You told me not to tell you."

"I guess I did at that."

"How's the wound feel?"

50

"It burns like hell. What'd you do?"

"I cauterized it with gunpowder."

"I'm real glad you didn't tell me. There's only one thing."

"What's that?"

"I heard gunpowder doesn't work."

"We'll see."

"You goin' to tell me what made them bastards open up on the cabin?"

"The sheriff was showing off. It's the gang's hideout, no doubt, but Blowser wanted to throw me off by firing into it, showing me how eager he was to get the highwaymen. But like I said, it was all for show. They were trying to impress me."

"Why bother to impress you?"

"Blowser knew I was a U.S. marshal."

"So?"

"I'm not the first federal marshal to come lookin' for his gang. The rest have disappeared, and I guess Blowser figured it would look better this time if I sent back glowing reports of what a fine lawman he was. Before I showed up, he was going to ride out with his 'posse' and make a big show of going after the highwaymen, but I showed up and joined his posse. It didn't take long for me to notice that all the members of the posse were old buddies and all of them with a bad case of the slows."

"And that's the Skull Canyon Gang chasing us now?"

"I'd be more certain if them two who worked me over the night you found me were riding with them."

"How do you know they weren't just drifters?"

"Maybe they were. But one thing is certain."

"What's that?"

"With what I know now, Sheriff Blowser can't let me live."

"Or me either."

"Afraid so, Jim."

Wells nodded wearily. "Well, I'll worry about that later. Right now I need some shut-eye."

He slumped to one side. Longarm stepped closer and helped the man to get comfortable on the cave's rocky floor. After muttering his thanks to Longarm, Wells was asleep almost at once. He covered Wells with his slicker, then took up his rifle and slipped from the cave. He descended the slope to the canyon floor and walked back along it until he reached the draw where he had left their horses.

It was a narrow, twisting draw, and Longarm had tethered the horses to a clump of scrub pine in under an overhanging lip of rock, invisible from the canyon. He approached the horses carefully, not wanting to spook them; he was being extremely cautious, since he could not be sure the posse had really left the area.

The horses were in fine shape, most of the grass at their feet cropped clean. They were thirsty, however, and Longarm emptied water from his canteen into his palm and gave each animal what he could spare, careful not to lose any fingers in the process. The mounts would have to wait until tomorrow for more. Longarm planned on moving out first thing in the morning, if Wells could handle it.

He unsaddled the horses, dumping the saddles under a tree, then left the horses and started back down the draw. He was almost out of it when he heard a rock rattling down the slope across from him and ducked back into the draw. A rifle shot cracked from the canyon rim opposite. The slug took a bite out of the canyon wall just over his head, showering him with rock shards. Keeping low, he peered out from the draw and saw Mike Smithers hunched behind a boulder on the canyon rim opposite. His pink face was wrinkled into a grin, his long white hair halolike in the bright sunlight. When he caught sight of Longarm, he fired again. Longarm ducked back as the bullet whined past him.

"Hey, there, Long!" Smithers cried. "You better throw out your weapon and come out of that draw with your hands up. We got you surrounded."

"Who's we?"

Instead of telling Longarm, Smithers sent another round into the draw, which told Longarm what he had guessed. This was going to be just between him and Smithers. The sheriff must have left Smithers behind while he and the rest of the posse continued to search the surrounding badlands.

Longarm turned about and studied the almost sheer walls of the draw. He wanted to get above Smithers, but only a bat could make it up these almost sheer rock walls. He peered out from behind a flanking curtain of rock at the canyon rim beyond.

Smithers had disappeared.

Longarm ducked out of the draw and loped swiftly across the canyon floor. Before he reached the far wall, Smithers began firing down on him from the lower portion of the slope. Longarm smiled. He had caught the son of a bitch scrambling down the canyon wall to get closer to the draw. As the ground around his feet began kicking up, Longarm scrambled up the side of the canyon until he was out of Smithers's line of sight. He kept on up the steep slope, twice using his rifle stock to keep himself from slipping back down. He had almost reached the canyon rim when he caught sight of Smithers running along the rim toward him in an effort to cut him down before he reached the top of the canyon wall.

Longarm held up long enough to send a rifle shot at Smithers, who immediately slewed to a stop and ducked low. Longarm continued on up the slope, vaulted onto the canyon's rim, and legged it for the protection of a couple of boulders squatting well back of the canyon rim. As soon as he reached them, he started to set up as Smithers appeared in full sight on his right, his rifle spitting.

Longarm flung himself to the ground behind a boulder and returned his fire, then felt a boot strike his wrist. As his rifle spun away, Longarm looked up to see Chet Breed leering down on him, his Colt cocked and ready.

"Freeze, bastard," said Breed, his yellow teeth gleaming in a smile.

Damn! Longarm had guessed wrong and run into the lion's mouth, head high and tail wagging. He could smell the man from where he crouched on the ground. That was probably the reason the sheriff had kept him back here with Smithers, who was advancing on Longarm now, breathing hard but happy at their catch, sweat pouring down his face—and no wonder, with those two cartridge belts folded across his chest.

"You sure made it easy for us," Smithers cried, halting a few feet from Longarm.

"Guess I did at that."

54

"Hot damn! Gil sure will be pleased. I told him you weren't far."

"Did you?"

"I knew that other one with you was hurt bad. So I figured you couldn't'a gone far."

"But he wouldn't listen, huh?" Longarm asked.

As he spoke, he sat up, causing both men to take an instinctive step backward.

"Hey, there," said Breed. "Watch it. Just stay put."

Without a word, Longarm scooted back against a boulder and appeared to relax. Breed looked over at Smithers.

"What do we do now?"

"Get the other one."

"He's dead," Longarm said. "You guys shot him up pretty bad."

Smithers grinned. "That so?"

"Fact is," said Breed, "we figure you're a lyin' son of a bitch, Marshal."

"Now, that's not nice, Chet," Smithers told his partner. "You ought to be more respectful. Don't forget. This here's a federal marshal—another poor bastard sent out from Washington."

"From Denver," Longarm said. "And if you finish me off, there'll be others."

Breed snorted as he glanced around at the desolate landscape. "Well, there's sure plenty of room for them poor bastards out here—and plenty of vultures looking for a good meal. That last federal marshal was big enough to keep them vultures stuffed for a week."

"He was a Pinkerton."

"That so?" Breed said. "We was wondering why he was so fat."

55

Longarm edged away from Breed. "Maybe the first thing you should do, Breed, is take a bath."

Breed's smile vanished. "Up yours, mister."

"Otherwise," continued Longarm, "if you go to sleep out here, them vultures might think you're already dead and start picking you over."

Smithers snickered. Longarm looked over at him. "Ain't that right, Smithers?"

Smithers looked at Breed and wrinkled his nose. "You do smell pretty rank, Breed," he said. "When's the last time you took a bath?"

Stung, Breed snapped, "That ain't none of your business."

"Was it last year or the year before?"

"Now, cut that shit out, Mike," snarled Breed. "I just sweat easy, that's all."

Smithers smiled. "Anyway, when we ride back to Iron City, it might be a good idea if you rode upwind of me."

Really upset now, Breed turned his full attention to Smithers, and was about to snarl a suitable retort when Longarm, having braced himself against the boulder, launched himself up off the ground and drove his left shoulder into Breed's right side, digging in hard. Breed uttered a small cry and buckled under Longarm's assault, his Colt clattering to the ground. As he staggered back, then sprawled headlong to the ground, Longarm spun about to see Smithers bringing up his rifle.

Longarm charged Smithers, ducked under the upraised rifle, and rammed him brutally in the chest, his head burrowing into the spot where the cartridge belts crossed. His hat went flying and his head protested as it crunched against the shells in the canvas belts, but he kept charging. The air exploded from Smithers's lungs and as he went reeling back, Longarm wrested the rifle from his grasp and spun around, his fierce momentum causing him to lose his balance.

He fell to the ground.

As he struck it, he saw that Breed was back on his feet and had drawn his sixgun. Longarm levered swiftly and fired at him. The slug caught Breed in the gut. He halted, surprised, and looked beyond Longarm at Smithers, as if Smithers were somehow responsible. Longarm rolled over. Smithers was still on his feet, reaching back for his sixgun. Leaping upright, Longarm swung the rifle stock like a baseball bat and caught Smithers on the side of his neck. The sound of crunching vertebrae echoed among the rocks and Smithers dropped the gun and crumpled to the ground, his neck broken, both eyes frozen open in surprise.

Longarm looked back at Breed.

The man was sitting on the ground holding his guts in both of his hands. He was trying to push them back in through the bloody hole in his pants. They were sleek, glistening gray coils flecked with blood, and with each breath Breed took, they surged relentlessly out past his filthy, clutching fingers. Considering how long a man's guts were, pushing them back in was a near-impossible assignment, and besides, Breed was in no condition to handle the job.

Tears in his eyes, Breed looked up at Longarm. "My God! Look what you done to me."

"Don't feel bad."

"Why not?"

"Like you said, there's plenty of buzzards out here looking for a good meal. Once them vultures get past the stink, they'll be sitting down to a real banquet. You and Smithers."

"Damn your eyes!"

"No sense in complaining. It's the best use you've been put to since your mother dropped you."

Without replying, Breed slipped slowly sideways. His hands relaxed, giving up the futile, useless battle. Before Longarm could lean past the awful stench of Breed's bowels to see if he was dead yet, Breed's head sagged lifelessly. Longarm straightened, picked up his hat and then his rifle, and headed back along the canyon's rim, anxious to reach the cave and rouse Jim Wells.

Despite his condition, Jim Wells would not be able to stay in the cave overnight to rest up. They would have to pull out now, before the sheriff returned to see what kind of luck Smithers and Breed might have had. If the sheriff found them before the buzzards, he'd know for sure they had caught up to Longarm.

Which meant their luck had been bad.

Chapter 5

Despite all the gunfire, Jim Wells was still asleep when Longarm reached the cave. Looking down at the unconscious man, Longarm realized how much better it would be for Jim Wells if Sheriff Blowser thought he had died as a result of his wounds. The sheriff could forget about him then and concentrate on Longarm. This would get Jim Wells out of this, and that was what Longarm wanted.

He left the cave and spent close to half an hour lugging boulders as he built a stone cairn on a ridge high above the cave. To make absolutely sure the posse members didn't miss it when they rode back through the canyon, he pounded a wooden cross into the ground in front of it and looped Wells's red bandanna over it. Then he returned to the draw and with a sharp crack to its rump sent Wells's horse off down the canyon.

Back in the cave, he shook Jim Wells awake and told him to ready himself for a long ride. Wells managed to climb up behind him, but before they could ride out, Longarm had to loop a rope around them both to prevent

Wells from falling off. They rode through the rest of that day, and it was close to midnight when they arrived at Ruth Osborne's ranch house. Longarm reined up in the yard. By the time he got Wells untied and had eased him off the horse, Wells was barely conscious.

The door to the cabin opened. Longarm glanced over to see Ruth standing in the doorway in her long nightdress, what looked like a double-barreled shotgun in her hand.

"Who's there?" she called.

Behind her in the doorway, her father lit a lantern, the shifting glow highlighting her slender form.

"It's me! Custis!" he called out to her. "I could use a hand."

"Are you hurt?" Ruth cried, running out into the night toward him.

"Not me, a friend of mine."

Barely supporting himself, Wells opened his eyes. "Where the hell are we?"

"At the Osborne ranch."

"What?"

"The same place you left me that night. Remember?"

"The same place?"

"One good turn deserves another."

"Oh, yeah . . . sure," he replied groggily.

Ruth and Ben had reached them by this time. Wells focused dazedly on Ruth's father and then Ruth.

"Ruth, Ben," Longarm said, "meet Jim Wells."

Frowning with concern, Ruth stepped quickly to Wells's side and flung his right arm over her shoulder. Her father, barefoot and dressed in red flannels, took Ruth's shotgun from her. As Ruth and Longarm helped the nearly unconscious Wells toward the house, Ben lit the way with his lantern.

"Into my bedroom," Ruth said when they reached the ranch house.

"Looks like you'll be giving up your bed for a while again," Longarm commented.

"How bad is Jim hurt?"

"Gunshot wound. In the left shoulder."

They reached her bedroom and carefully eased Wells onto her bed. He was still barely conscious, but as soon as he felt the mattress jouncing gently under him, his eyes closed and he passed out. Ben began to undress him. Satisfied Wells was in good hands, Longarm left the bedroom and was at the outside door when Ruth overtook him.

"Where are you going?"

"I'm heading out."

"But can't you stay here for now? You look exhausted."

"I am. Now look, I don't want you to get involved in this business, so tell Ben not to go into town until this is over."

"Dad?"

"As you said, he likes to wet his whistle."

"But what . . . ?" And then she realized what Longarm meant. "You mean he might—"

"I mean whiskey loosens his tongue, and if he lets on that Jim Wells is here, it could endanger him—and you too."

"Custis, what is this all about?"

"I found the Skull Canyon Gang."

"Then why don't you tell the sheriff?"

61

"Because Blowser is their leader."

"Gil Blowser?"

"You heard me."

"My God, Custis!"

"So keep Ben at home."

"Of course."

"For now anyway."

"But where are you going now?"

"To Rim Rock. I might not be able to wire my chief from Iron City. And I'm ready to admit that I'll need some help bringing in these bastards."

Longarm started out the door.

"Custis?"

He turned.

"Be careful."

"You too."

She leaned close then and kissed him on the lips. He held her for a long moment, relishing the clean nighttime freshness of her—hating it that he was leaving her again so soon. When he rode into the yard a moment before, it had seemed like he was coming home after a long, weary assignment. But the assignment wasn't over yet. It had really only just begun.

He released her, kissed her on the forehead gently, then turned and hurried back out to his horse and mounted up. He swung his horse around and rode out of the yard. When he looked back, she was still standing in the doorway.

He waved.

Before dawn Longarm was crossing a boulder-pocked valley when he came upon an abandoned settler's shack, a one-room affair built into the side of a hill, its two sides fashioned of unpeeled logs and chinked with mud. The winter snows and many rains had washed most of the chinking away, and the old piece of cowhide serving as a door was in tatters.

Dismounting, Longarm led his horse into the nearby lean-to, unsaddled his mount, then headed for the shack. He ripped down the cowhide and stepped into the shack's cool interior. There was a cot in one corner. It needed cleaning off, but Longarm was too exhausted to attend to it. He was asleep a moment after he kicked off his boots and stretched out on it.

The next day, the mid-afternoon sun burning a brand on his back, he rode into a thick stand of willows and cottonwoods lining a nearly dry streambed. He was almost to the bank of the stream when he glimpsed through the trees a settler's covered wagon stalled on the other side of the streambed. The settler had pulled up his flatbed beside the wagon, and its two horses along with those pulling the covered wagon were still standing in their traces, the four horses looking so completely beaten down by the sun that they had lost even the will to flick their tails at the flies bedeviling them.

The settler and his two women, busy trying to fix the wagon, hadn't caught sight of him yet. From their dress and the bedraggled, defeated look about them, Longarm figured they were Latter-day Saints. Longarm dismounted, unsaddled the chestnut, and hobbled it close to the thin trickle of water still meandering close under the bank. Then he left the cottonwoods and trudged out into the sun and across the riverbed's polished gravel to the three Mormons clustered behind the wagon.

He saw the trouble immediately. The wooden rim on the wagon's left rear wheel had shrunk in the dry heat, causing the iron tire to peel off. A dark-clad Mormon, sweat pouring down his face, had just finished attempting to lift the wagon so his women could pull the wheel off the axle. He was a big man, but he didn't have near the heft he would need to lift the wagon high enough. Judging from the condition of the horses he was allowing to stand in their traces, and his stupidity in trying to lift the wagon through sheer brute strength, this Mormon settler struck Longarm as even more inept that the average sodbuster. As Longarm approached, the Mormon made no effort to greet him. As far as he knew, Longarm was afoot, and a man afoot in this country could not be worth much.

Longarm pulled up beside the Mormon and his two women, said nothing, and watched.

His feet planted solidly on the ground, his back pressed hard against the rear of the wagon, the Mormon grabbed hold of the underside of the wagon's bed, cursed the two women to get their attention, then warned them that if they didn't pull the goddamn wheel off this time, he'd have their hides. Then he closed his eyes and made another desperate heave upward.

The two women—one a pretty blonde about twenty or so, the other a heftier, more solid female in her early thirties—tugged desperately on the wheel. But it was hopeless. The wheel was wedged deep into the ground, and no matter how hard they struggled to pull it free, they were not going to pull it off the axle unless they could figure a way to lower the earth about two feet at the same time their lord and master lifted the wagon.

With a bellow of frustration, the exhausted Mormon let his burden drop. With a silent nod of greeting to the man, Longarm walked past him and peered into the rear of the wagon. As he had expected, he found it piled high with household goods. He saw a massive bureau, bed frames, dressers, trunks, and poking through all this the edge of a sewing machine. There were other items too numerous to count. Stepping away from the wagon, Longarm looked at the exhausted, red-faced Mormon.

The man was mopping his face and neck with a black kerchief as he stared balefully at Longarm. He was a tall, gaunt man with beetling brows, a large, hooked blade of a nose, and eyes almost as black as an Indian's.

"I'm Walter Keefer," the Mormon told Longarm, without offering his hand. "And who might you be?"

"Custis Long."

"You afoot?"

"I left my horse in the shade of them cottonwoods," Longarm replied. "Where your horses ought to be."

"I don't need your advice."

"Maybe not," Longarm replied. "But you sure as hell need someone to tell you how to lift that wagon so you can pull off that wheel."

"You tellin' me I don't know my business?"

"If your business is fitting loose tires back onto wheels, I'd say yes."

The two women, cowed and sweating miserably in the terrible heat, had straightened up warily to watch as Longarm approached their husband. Now, at Longarm's blunt words, they pulled back in astonishment—as if they expected their master to rise up in all his Power and Glory and smite Longarm on the spot.

But Keefer only kept on mopping his face and neck with his bandanna. "All right, mister," he said, "just how would *you* go about it?"

"I'd empty the wagon first."

"Every item?" Keefer seemed dismayed at the thought.

"That's right. Every goddamn thing you got in there."

Keefer turned to his two women. "Well, you heard him."

The two women set to work. Longarm expected Keefer to give them a hand, but he contented himself with watching impatiently as they struggled, his arms folded imperiously over his chest. Longarm shook his head in disgust and walked back across the riverbed to a spot in the timber where he had noticed a downed cottonwood limb. Picking it up by one end, he dragged it across the gravel all the way out to the wagon. The two women were still at work, still lugging the household goods out onto the ground. He watched them struggle with the sewing machine, straining mightily so as not to drop it, and could stand it no longer. He hurried over and gave them a hand with it, then climbed into the wagon to help them with the rest of the furniture. Shamed into it, Keefer pitched in himself, his face dark with annoyance.

Once the wagon was emptied, Longarm fitted one end of the branch snugly under the wagon's rear axle, then thrust his shoulder under the other end. He beckoned to the older of the two women. She approached Longarm hesitantly, her eyes darting nervously at Keefer.

"Go ahead," Keefer snapped, having by now perceived Longarm's intent. "Hurry up and get over there. Do like he says."

The woman moved quickly up beside Longarm.

"Now this won't be hard," Longarm assured her. "Just put your shoulders under this end here next to me and when I give the word, heave upward."

Hastily brushing her matted hair off her shoulders, she took her place beside him, tucking her shoulder under the limb snugly against his.

"All right, Keefer," Longarm told him, "get over to that wheel and pull it off when we lift."

Apparently seething inwardly at Longarm's manner, but reluctant to lose this chance to get out of his present difficulties, the Mormon crouched down beside the wheel and took hold of it with both hands. Longarm glanced at the woman.

"On three. Ready?"

She nodded.

"One—two—*three*!"

They both heaved upward. The branch bent slightly, then held, and the axle and wagon lifted into the air. The wheel began to turn freely. Keefer tugged once, twice— and the wheel slid off the end of the axle. As soon as he dragged it away from the wagon, Longarm nodded to the woman and they eased the wagon back to the ground.

"My, you made that so easy," the woman whispered, gazing up into Longarm's eyes.

This close to her, he could see that despite her sweaty, disheveled appearance, she was a handsome woman, light-skinned, with dark brown eyes and a light smattering of freckles. She was so handsome, Longarm could not help wonder what in hell had prompted her to become this hapless Mormon's wife.

He dropped the branch, walked over to Keefer, and looked down at the wagon wheel resting on the ground.

Keefer appeared uncertain as to what to do next.

"You'll need a water hole to soak it in after you put the tire back on," Longarm told him.

"I know that," Keefer snapped.

"So what's the problem?"

"There's not near enough water along here. I need to cover the wheel completely."

"There may be a water hole further upstream."

"You know that for sure, do you?"

"No."

"Well, then?"

"I say it's worth a try."

"I say you're crazy."

Longarm glanced over at the flatbed wagon simmering in the sun, the two unhappy horses standing in its traces close to collapse. "I tell you what," Longarm said to Keefer. "I'll load the wheel and tire onto the flatbed over there, and drive up the river a ways. If there's a water hole, we'll find it and put the tire back on."

Keefer shrugged, offering no further objection. Longarm lugged the wheel and iron tire rim over to the flatbed and dumped them into the truck's bed. Longarm took off his Stetson and brushed the sweat off his forehead with the back of his wrist.

"If I find a water hole," Longarm said to Keefer, "I'll need some help when I get there."

Keefer glanced at the young girl. She was as slim as a poplar, with golden hair and blue eyes—obviously the master's new favorite. He turned then and squinted through the sunlight at the woman who had just helped Longarm lift the wagon.

"Matty," he said. "Go with him."

Matty nodded obediently.

"While we're gone," Longarm told Keefer, "I think you'd better unharness these two horses wilting in their traces and take them over to the cottonwoods before they collapse. There's a trickle of water close by the bank, near where I've hobbled my own mount. There should be enough water there for them."

Longarm's tone infuriated the Mormon. He stared balefully at Longarm for a moment, the veins on his forehead standing out, his eyes smoldering. But he said nothing as he flung himself about and started for the horses.

Matty at his side, Longarm walked over to the flatbed and led the team across the gravel to the thin trickle of water near the far bank. After the horses had slaked their thirst, Longarm checked to make sure his chestnut was doing all right. Then he and Matty climbed up onto the flatbed's seat. Matty took up the reins and headed downstream, keeping close by the bank.

As soon as they were out of sight of her husband and the covered wagon, Matty glanced over at him. "You near got yourself kilt back there," she told him.

"You mean your husband?"

She nodded grimly. "He's an Avenging Angel."

"That so?"

"And he don't mess with those who don't show him no respect. You better be careful, Mr. Long."

Longarm knew all he cared to know about the Avenging Angels, a band of night riders organized by Brigham Young. Their mission was to keep members of the Mormon Church in line. Any settler who failed to pay his tithe to the Church or who challenged the Church's authority on any matter of doctrine would be hauled off some moonless night by the Avenging Angels, never to be seen or heard of again. There was no mistaking the genuine fear Longarm had caught in Matty's voice, and Longarm was not unfamiliar with the terror the name of the Avenging Angels could arouse in the breast of any Mormon. As Longarm suspected, it was the chilling efficiency of these grim night riders that accounted for the Mormons' growing wealth and prosperity as well as for their marvelous church discipline and unity of thought on matters of creed.

"Well, I'm not a Mormon, Matty."

"That don't make no difference to him."

"It does to me. Maybe he better realize that there's a big world outside the Mormon world."

"But he don't, and that's a fact."

"No, I guess not. Your Lord and Master doesn't strike me as being all that bright."

She sighed. "He was a grocer at Windup. But now he's determined to find himself a homestead and live off the fat of the land."

"This land has very little fat on it, Matty."

She nodded in somber agreement. "Just whitened bones and dust—and rock."

"Which makes homesteading out here sound kind of foolish."

"It is."

"So why do it?"

"Ain't you heard what the Prophet said? We got to make the desert bloom."

"Easy for him to say."

"Maybe so, but Walter is determined to do it."

"You mean he's determined that you two women do it."

"I know," she said wearily. "And I don't expect Virginia to be much help."

"She the other wife?"

Matty nodded. "Walter just married her a while back. He's real taken with her right now, and don't like to see her work too hard—not right now anyway."

"Must be handy for him—having two wives, I mean."

"It is handy, Mr. Long. But not the way you think."

"How so?"

"You were thinking about it from a man's point of view. I'd rather think of what it means for the woman."

"And what *does* it mean?"

"Someone to help her with the chores. And the cooking. A friend to visit with and confide in when all those around her are men—big, stinking loudmouth animals stompin' and swearin' and lettin' out farts."

Longarm laughed. "I never thought of it like that."

"Well, you should. Homesteadin' can get pretty lonely for a woman, especially when her only companion is a man—"

"Like Keefer."

"Yes. Like Keefer."

"How are you and Virginia getting along?"

"So far, not so good. I was hoping she'd be a friend and pitch in with the work. But she ain't much help, after all. The only thing she wants is to sleep with Walter and present him with little Walters."

"That doesn't bother you?"

"What do you mean?"

71

"I mean your husband sleepin' with another woman."

She looked at him. "Walter is a dirty man, Mr. Long. A *very* dirty man. His stench makes my stomach turn, an' he makes love the way a dog shits. It ain't no pleasure to suffer under that heavin', sweatin' son of a bitch."

"I guess you don't mind then."

"Mind? If Virginia doesn't do a lick of work, she's done enough if she just keeps that animal off me."

Longarm asked no more questions.

They lifted into less dry country, and Longarm noticed that the grass growing along both banks was becoming thicker, the trees more plentiful. It was not long before they came to a wide, meandering loop in the streambed enclosed by a thick stand of cottonwoods, willows, and some oaks. Soon, ahead of them through the trees, they caught the shimmering gleam of a water hole. They kept on, and before long Matty pulled the team to a halt beside the water hole. They had traveled less than three miles, Longarm reckoned, but here was all the water they would need.

Longarm jumped down and, with Matty's help, lifted the wheel and iron tire out of the wagon and rolled them into a shallow portion of the water hole. Longarm took off his boots and socks, rolled up his pants, and waded out into the water. Matty hitched her long dress up her knees and splashed in after him, and together they fitted the iron tire onto the wheel's wooden rim, then let the wheel sink into the shallow water.

Then they clambered back up onto the bank and made themselves comfortable while they waited for the water to swell the wooden rim enough to make it fast to the tire. They were close to a sheeperry bush, so Matty began picking the berries, using her skirt as a basket. Longarm leaned back on his elbows, and was beginning to relax some when he became aware of the distant thunder of hoofbeats. He got to his feet and hurried back through the timber. He paused at the edge to peer out.

A familiar posse was approaching. He watched them long enough to be sure they were heading for the water hole, then hurried back to Matty.

"We got visitors."

"Who?"

"A sheriff and his posse. He's looking for me. I'm going to duck under the flatbed over there." He unholstered his Colt and checked its load. "If any shooting starts, get in the water and keep your head down."

"Don't be silly," Matty told him. "They'll see you under that wagon in a minute. We'll both be killed if any shooting starts. Give me that Colt."

"You crazy? You can't shoot it out with this posse."

"I know that. Now give me your Colt."

Longarm handed the Colt to her. "You know how to use it?"

"Of course. Now get under my skirt."

"What?"

"You hard of hearing? Get your head and shoulders under my skirt and stretch your feet out under the bush."

"That's crazy."

"All of you won't fit under the bush. But your head and shoulders will fit under my skirt. Hurry!"

Longarm hesitated, but the pound of approaching hooves concentrated his thinking wonderfully. Matty was right. Under that wagon he'd be spotted for sure, and he was too big a man to be concealed entirely by the bush. As Matty began mussing her hair and daubing mud over her face, he took off his hat and ducked under her skirt, squirmed around so that his head and shoulders rested back against her belly, then thrust his legs out until his boots were out of sight under the bush.

Concealing the Colt in a fold of her skirt, Matty moved slightly to make herself more comfortable. Spreading her thighs, she pressed his head down between them. He felt the back of his head resting against her crotch, and realized for the first time that she was wearing nothing under her dress. When he tried to lift his head slightly, she placed her hand on his forehead to keep him where he was.

"Stay still!" she whispered urgently. "Please. They're coming through the trees now!"

Chapter 6

Longarm could remember some compromising positions he had been caught in before, but this one took first place. What made it worse was the fact that he had to remain where he was and sweat it out. As he unclipped his derringer from the watch-fob chain, he could hear the shuddering pounding of the posse's hoofbeats as they rode on straight for Matty.

"Well, now, ma'am," said Blowser, his mount blowing as the sheriff yanked it to a halt. "What've we got here?"

Blowser seemed so close, Longarm's hand tightened on his derringer.

"You blind, mister?"

Blowser's horse shook its head, causing the bit to jingle some; the sound came from almost directly over Longarm's head.

"You mean that's what you're doin'? Pickin' berries?"

"That and more, mister."

"What else then?"

"You blind? Look in the water. We got a busted wheel. I'm waiting for the wood to swell so the tire will stay on."

The chink of the sheriff's spurs sounded only a few feet from Longarm's head as the sheriff dismounted, walked past Matty, and peered down into the water hole. After a pause, he turned and walked back to his horse. Longarm braced himself, acutely aware of the snorting and stamping of the rest of the posse's horses not twenty paces away as the sheriff's men sat their horses and watched.

"Lost a tire, did you?" Blowser asked Matty.

"You seen it, didn't you?" she retorted sharply.

"Yeah, we seen it," said Tim O'Malley from his horse, his tone derisive, as usual.

"Something you gents should know," Matty said. "My husband's wagon train is not far from here. He'll be expectin' me back with this tire pretty soon now."

"You got me shiverin' in my boots," drawled O'Malley.

The sheriff chuckled. "You ain't got to fear us none, ma'am. I'm Sheriff Blowser, and this here's a legal posse. Besides, we're lookin' for a Gentile, not a Mormon."

"You won't find no Gentiles around me."

"Well, now, hold on a minute. You might've seen him ridin' by. He's forkin' a big chestnut."

"Never seen him."

"You answered that mighty quick," snapped O'Malley.

Longarm could imagine the one-eyed pirate leaning over his saddlehorn to get a closer look at Matty, his eye fixed malevolently on her, the smoke from his cigarette coiling past his eye patch, a fearsome visage that had to make Matty more than a little nervous.

"I told you," she responded without a quaver. "I didn't see any rider. I been too busy with this damn wheel."

"I say we water our horses," said Will Coombs, his voice coming from the right, "fill our canteens, and move out, Gil. I want to get this thing over with. We been pounding our asses on these saddles too damn long already."

"Now, hold on a just a cotton-pickin' minute," said Wilson. "Let's hang around a while." There was a leer in the deputy's voice.

"Why?" demanded the sheriff.

"You blind, Sheriff? Lookit what we got here to play with—a big husky Mormon woman. She has to share her man with other women. Don't you think we should show her what some real men could do for her?"

"You outa your head?" demanded O'Malley.

"Yeah, look at her," said Hound unhappily. "Why, you'd have to throw a sack over her head to really enjoy it."

"I ain't interested in her head," barked Wilson.

"Cut that talk," said the sheriff. "O'Malley's right. We got other business to tend to now. We got to catch that bastard that kilt Breed and Smithers."

"Aw, shit," said Wilson. "It's been a long time for me."

"For all of us," agreed Hound sadly. He seemed to have reconsidered his earlier objection. "There ain't no tellin' how long this here chase'll go on."

"It'll go on as long as it takes," barked the sheriff.

"We got to find that bastard, or it'll be our ass. The son of a bitch knows too much."

"I was just thinkin' that a little ass might refresh us some," persisted Wilson, snickering.

"Yeah, give us more incentive," said Hound.

"Never thought of that," said Will Coombs. "It might be just the thing."

"Hound," Wilson suggested, "I think if you wash off some of that dirt on her face, you might find she don't look so bad."

"I say she's right pretty," said Will Coombs.

It was clear that the longer the posse members contemplated the apparently defenseless Mormon woman sitting on the ground before them, the more appealing she became. Longarm expected to hear O'Malley join the chorus before long.

"Hell! You better face it, Gil," said Coombs. "We got you outvoted on this one."

"Three against two," said Hound.

O'Malley spoke up then, the sarcastic cut of his words stinging them. "All right, you horny bastards. Go ahead. Get to it. I might like a piece of that myself. But make it fast."

"Yeah," said the sheriff resignedly, "we don't have much time."

Spurred boots struck the ground as the posse members dismounted hurriedly, the chink of their spurs growing louder as they approached Matty—and Longarm.

"Now you listen here," Matty warned them. "Stay back, I say!"

"Just relax," purred Wilson.

"Yeah, we ain't aimin' to hurt you none," Will

Coombs assured her. "We're just takin' a few more slices off the loaf."

"Sure," said Hound. "Might as well lean back and enjoy it."

"I'm warning you!" Matty cried. "My husband is an Avenging Angel!"

"Hold up, men," said the sheriff. "We don't want to tangle with them Mormon night riders."

"Aw, hell, Sheriff," said Wilson. "You scare too easy."

"Besides, she was just bluffin'," said Will Coombs hopefully.

"Look at it this way," said Hound eagerly. "Her old man's probably got a roomful of wives just waitin' to take her place. He won't notice if she's a little tired. I hear tell Mormon husbands keep real harems—like the Turks."

The men shuffled closer. Through the nearly suffocating folds of Matty's dress, Longarm could hear their heavy breathing, and had no difficulty at all imagining the leers on their faces.

Hound spoke up then. "I got an idea, men."

"Well?"

"Why don't we just take her with us?"

"You crazy?"

"I'm sick of cookin' for you animals. You ain't got no appreciation of good food. She could cook, an' then take care of us at night. Be a real pleasure to have a woman around."

"We ain't ridin' with no woman," snapped the sheriff.

"That's all right," said Wilson. "You don't need to

have anything to do with her, Blowser. You can watch."

The gang laughed and slapped their thighs at that. It was clear they had come to a decision. Matty was going with them as their cook—among other chores. Longarm felt Matty shudder. And he didn't blame her. The posse was so close by this time that he was almost overwhelmed by the powerful stench they gave off, one compounded of unwashed armpits and loins mixed with that of horses and sixguns.

Longarm gripped his derringer tightly, getting himself ready to leap out from Matty's skirts. His hope was that surprise combined with the derringer would give him enough of an edge to make a decent fight of it. Perhaps Matty would be able to get off a few shots herself. It was a hopeless, desperate resolve, and would most likely result in their death, but they had no choice in the matter.

Longarm tensed his muscles and prepared to jump to his feet. Before he could, Matty snatched up the Colt in her lap and fired. Its detonation was so close and thunderous it set Longarm's ears to ringing—and after it came Matty's voice, sharp and commanding.

"That was a warning shot, gents. Come a step closer, and I'll blow your balls off."

"Hey!" cried Hound, his voice shaking in terror.

"Jesus," breathed Wilson.

Longarm heard the posse members scrambling hastily back.

"Go easy with that cannon, ma'am," the sheriff warned. "No need to get all riled."

"Well, I am riled!"

The Colt roared again in Matty's hand. Longarm heard

Hound scream in pain and terror, after which came the sound of him leaping into his saddle and riding off, squealing like a stuck pig.

"You almost kilt him!" cried the sheriff.

"I only shot his hat off, that's all. I did it a'purpose to show you I know how to aim this blame thing!"

"All right. All right. We believe you."

"Good. Now get the hell out of here, all of you!"

Longarm heard the squeak of saddle leather as the sheriff mounted up. "You made your point, ma'am. We'll just water our horses and fill our canteens. Then we'll be on our way."

"Not here you won't."

"Where then?"

"On the other side of these trees."

"Yeah, sure."

"And stay in sight so I can keep an eye on you."

Longarm heard the others mounting up, then ride off back through the trees. The pounding of their hooves did not vanish completely until they had reached the other side of the water hole. Longarm, drenched in perspiration, remained under Matty's skirt.

"How far away are they?" he asked softly.

"Shh . . . I can see each one of them."

"Keep that Colt ready."

"Don't worry none. I surely will."

Longarm could hear dimly the distant clink of canteens as the men filled them, and the sound of the horses splashing in the water as they drank their fill. After what felt like a century, he heard the jingle of bits as the men forked their mounts.

"You can put that gun away, ma'am!" Sheriff Blowser

called over to her. "We're clearin' out now!"

"I'll believe it when I see it," she shouted back at them. "Now, git!"

Longarm heard the sudden beat of hooves as the men wheeled their mounts and galloped off. Matty waited a decent interval, then stood up to watch them go. Longarm got to his feet also. All he could see was the dust raised by the posse's horses. And when it settled, they were gone.

"You did famously," Longarm said.

"I didn't want to shoot, but I could feel you getting ready to jump up."

"You're right. I was just going to."

"Here," she said shakily, handing the .44 back to him.

As he took it from her, he noticed that her cheeks had suddenly lost all their color. She was as white as a linen bed sheet.

"Mr. Long," she said in a tiny voice. "I think I'm goin' to faint."

She was as good as her word. Her eyes closed and she sagged forward into Longarm's arms. He lowered her gently to the ground. Alarmed, he holstered his .44, then soaked his bandanna in the water hole and dabbed at her forehead and cheeks with it. He then folded it neatly and rested it down on her forehead. Gradually the color returned to her face and she stirred slightly. Opening her eyes, she tried to sit up, but he pressed her gently back down.

"Just rest easy," he told her. "Give yourself time to recover."

She nodded obediently and lay back down.

"I was so scared," she told him, her voice hushed.

"You sure didn't show it."

"But I was. I knew what would happen if they got holt of me."

"I wouldn't have let them, Matty."

"That's all I could think of—you jumping up and bullets flying!"

"Like I said, you did fine. Matter of fact, you saved both our lives. How bad did you shoot Hound?"

"Was that his name?"

"Yes."

"He sure looked like a hound—a big, mournful droop-eared hound. I took his hat off and creased his skull some. But the way he screeched and rode off, I don't figure he's hurt all that bad."

Longarm chuckled. "You just scared the shit out of him, that's all. Looks to me like you're a crack shot."

"Oh, that second shot was just an accident, Custis. I was trembling so, I pulled too hard on the trigger."

Longarm chuckled. "Doesn't matter. You did fine. They won't soon forget you."

"They were horrible men. Why are they after you?"

"That's just it," Longarm told her. "I'm after *them*. Only they don't know it yet."

"All of them?"

"All five."

"There were more than five."

"How many more?"

She sat up slowly and took his damp bandanna off her forehead. She appeared as good as new. His damp bandanna had wiped most of the grime off her face and she did indeed look right handsome.

"Two more."

"You mean seven in all?"

"Yes."

"That's two more than I figured."

"There were two men who hung back. They grinned a lot, and I could see they was just as anxious as the others to join in when the time came, but they didn't say a word."

"Can you describe them?"

"They were filthy. One of them reminded me of a toad. He wore a derby hat and a filthy sheepskin coat."

"Torn?"

"It was in tatters."

"And the other one was a crazy-looking fellow, tall and lean as a rake handle, a mean look on his face."

"Yes. That's him, all right."

"The tall one's name is Ely, the short fat one is Windy Smith. I been lookin' for them too. I figured they might be a part of this gang, and I was right."

"It's over now, thank God."

"How do you feel?"

"Much better."

"Then maybe we'd better rescue that wheel before it drowns."

She laughed.

The wheel had absorbed so much moisture by this time that it took both of them to heave it up onto the flatbed. But the water hole had done its job. The iron tire was solidly fixed to the wooden rim, its edge biting sharply into the wooden rim.

On the way back, Longarm took the reins, and when

they came in sight of Keefer and Virginia waiting beside the covered wagon for them, Matty reached over and pulled on the reins.

"Pull up here, Mr. Long. Please?"

Longarm did as she bid. "What is it?"

"By the time we get this tire back on, it'll be close to sundown. Won't you stay with us tonight? We'll probably camp close by in the cottonwoods."

"No. I'll be moving on. It's cooler traveling by night."

"Where you headed?"

"Rim Rock."

"That's where we're headin' too."

"So maybe I'll see you again."

"That's not soon enough. Why don't you camp tonight at that spot we just came from? You don't have to stay there all night. You could just rest up for a while."

"Now, Matty, why should I do that?"

She tipped her head, her eyes gleaming mischievously. "Mr. Long, you mean you really don't know?"

"But you're married. What about your husband?"

Matty took his hand in hers. "You remember what that one said back there? About it being a long time for him? Well, Mr. Long, it's been a long time for me too. And I can still feel your head resting back against me down there. Every time I think of it, my knees go weak."

Longarm had already had occasion to judge the solid heft of her thighs and to smell the hot musky perfume of her crotch. It had been a long time for him as well, he reckoned.

"All right. How will you get to me?"

"I'll walk."

"You won't have to. See that low ridge?"

She followed his gaze. "I see it."

"I'll be waiting behind it—we can ride double on my chestnut."

"That would be nice."

"There's just one thing."

"Yes?"

"What'll your Lord and Master be doing while all this is going on?"

"He'll be sleepin' with Virginia, as usual." She shuddered slightly. "Poor girl."

Without further comment, Longarm slapped the reins, and the team started up again.

Not long after the light in the covered wagon went out, Longarm was reaching down to haul Matty up behind him. As they rode back to his campsite, she rested her cheek against his back, her arms twined tightly about him, and as soon as they reached the water hole, she slipped down off the chestnut. Flinging off her dress, she plunged into the water.

Longarm hobbled the chestnut, unsaddled it, undressed, and dove into the water beside her. The desert night was chill, but the water retained much of the day's warmth, and for a while he and Matty frolicked in the water like overgrown kids. Then they scrambled ashore and flung themselves down on Longarm's waiting bedroll. As Longarm hit, he reached up and tried to grab her.

Laughing, she pushed him away so she could wring out her hair. He leaned back to wait not so patiently as she combed out her long hair, using only her fingers. Soon her shimmering tresses curled down over her breasts, while the wet pubic patch gleaming between her lush thighs winked at him like a dark jewel.

His patience gone, he reached for her again. This time she didn't pull back, but came at him as eagerly as he, their mouths colliding, their lips pulling and sucking at each other. Longarm's arms tightened about her, and soon he was prowling hungrily over her. Eagerly she opened wide for him, pulling him down and into her. He plunged down and sank deep, so deep that for a while he thought he'd never find bottom.

One thing led swiftly to another and after a frenzied bit of lovemaking, the two—panting, laughing, and pleased as hell with each other—lay back and looked up at the moonless skies bending over them, the stars a profuse, milky necklace of light.

"Oh, that was so good, Mr. Long."

"Call me Custis."

"I guess I should, shouldn't I?"

"Well, I'd say we're pretty well acquainted by now."

"We certainly are, Custis."

He propped himself up onto his elbow and gazed at her full-sized, ample womanhood, the full breasts and then the dip of her waist, followed by the lush, upwelling sweep of her thighs. She was all woman. That poor asshole Keefer was losing out on a very fine woman.

But of course, he would never know that.

Matty groped for his crotch and found he was ready to go again. She laughed in delight, pushed him onto his back, and mounted him eagerly. Little sounds came from her. She called his name over and over. He tried to hold back to give her more pleasure, but before long she was pulling him along after her and he let go as her gasps grew stronger, her head swung wildly from right to left.

"Now, oh, now!" she cried in a kind of half sob.

Her hands became fists as she beat on his chest. He laughed up at her and at the stars and came just as she did, the two of them erupting joyously, miraculously, together. She collapsed heavily down onto him, her forehead slamming into his collarbone.

"Oh, I didn't mean that," she cried. "Are you all right? Did I hurt you?"

"I'm fine," he said with a laugh.

He held her close then and rolled over onto her. He cupped one of her warm pillowy breasts in his hands and closed his lips about the nipple, then rested his head in her sweaty cleft. She rested her hand on the side of his head and pressed him gently against her, sighing in contentment.

"I guess that'll keep me," she murmured happily.

"Me too."

Soon, with Matty cradling Longarm's head in her breasts, they napped for a while, then played around some more, until Longarm looked up and saw the position of the dipper.

"Time to go," he said.

She sighed. "I was afraid of that."

She sat up and looked around her. "Oh, dear! Where's my dress? I was in such a hurry to get out of it!"

She found it quickly enough and soon, humming softly, she climbed up onto the chestnut behind Longarm. As she wrapped her arms around his waist again, she kissed him on the neck. The ride back through the cool, moonlit night was pleasant and sad all at the same time.

She slipped down off his horse and looked up at him. "That was so nice, Custis."

"Yes, it was."

She lifted her face up to him for one last kiss. He kissed her, then held his chestnut in check as he watched her hurry toward the cottonwoods. A moment before she reached them, she turned and waved to him. He waved back, then set the chestnut in motion. Meeting up with the Mormon settler and his two women had sure worn him out. But he wasn't complaining any. Matty had saved his life, then hauled his ashes. There was no doubt about it, she was some woman. But what a waste for her to be married to that fool of a Mormon.

As he rode on through the night, he found himself whistling softly to himself.

Chapter 7

"You heard me, mister. The lines are down. I can't send no telegram."

Longarm stared at the telegrapher, then out the window past him at the railroad tracks gleaming in the morning sunlight and the telegraph poles reaching as far as the eye could see.

"How long they been out?"

"Since yesterday afternoon," the old-timer said, snugging down his battered rebel cap. He was clearly as distressed as Longarm to have his lines down.

"Is there a crew out lookin' for the break?"

"Course, there is."

"Since when?"

The old man stood up and peered out the window as if he expected to see the repair linesmen gliding up the track on their rail cart at that very minute. "They been gone since yesterday," he said, "but the lines are still down."

"I'll be back later then."

"It ain't my fault, mister. This ain't happened only once before—in the '78 blizzard."

"That's all right. Like I said, I'll be back later."

The old man slumped back down to stare at his silent keys and chucked his rebel cap back off his forehead. He looked as unhappy as a heavy drinker at closing time.

Outside, Longarm led the chestnut away from the station's hitch rack and swung up into the saddle, then headed across the tracks and down the single main street, aware that Sheriff Blowser had been just a step ahead of him on this one. It must have been the sheriff who cut the lines to keep Longarm from telegraphing Vail.

It was a little after ten in the morning and Rim Rock's main street was crowded with covered wagons, part of a Mormon stream of settlers surging into the area. The sight of the Latter-day Saints depressed Longarm as he trotted past their wagons. Most of the women had stony-faced, grim expressions, while their menfolk seemed to be bearded, wild-eyed fanatics, nearly all of them gaunt and hungry-looking—as if they had been cut from the same bleak stock. And then there were the children. Somber miniatures of their black-clad parents, they poked their heads out of the rear of the wagons, their hollow eyes staring out at the stores and passing horsemen. Longarm got the impression that for them, Mormon childhood was a kind of gray, cheerless prison.

At the first intersection, Longarm came to the four-story Palace Hotel. Alongside it was the Palace Saloon, and across the street the town's livery stable. Longarm rode up to the stable, and the hostler's dim figure materialized in its entrance as Longarm dismounted. Longarm slaked his thirst at the pipe gushing into the street trough and let his horse take its fill, after which he led the horse up the barn's wooden ramp.

"Second stall back," the hostler told him.

In the stall Longarm untied his bedroll, then unsaddled the horse. Slinging his saddlebags over his shoulder, he took his Winchester from its sling, and walked out of the livery. As he passed the hostler, he told him to feed the chestnut fresh oats and give it a rubdown.

He stood on the street for a moment, feeling a sudden, bone-deep weariness wash over him. He had been in the saddle since midnight and could feel every mile. He squared his shoulders and walked across the street to the hotel. He made sure the room assigned to him was on the top floor, high enough to muffle the street noises. He pushed into the room, kicked the door shut behind him, and locked it. He hung his hat on a bedpost and dumped his gear into a corner, then dropped onto the bed, hitting it like a log. He managed to kick off his boots, turned his head, and was asleep before the bed finished jouncing under him.

The sun had almost dropped behind the peaks to the west when Longarm awoke. He had slept through the worst heat of the day and was crawling with sweat. He didn't like the way he smelled. He got up, pulled on his boots, crossed to the washstand, and poured the tepid water from the pitcher into the washbowl. He lowered his face over it and with his bare hands washed off the mask of alkali dust that still clung to his face and neck. A rough muslin towel hung on a hook by the washstand, and he used it to dig the sand out of his ears and the corners of his eyes. As he dried himself off, he promised himself that as soon as he got some food in his stomach, he'd visit the barbershop and spend a while in a hot, scalding tub. He checked his hardware, snugged his hat down firmly, and headed for the door.

An hour later, fed and barbered, Longarm strode into the Palace Saloon to varnish his tonsils. He ordered a shot of Maryland rye, and was irritated to find there wasn't any whiskey or bourbon in stock.

"Well, what *do* you have?" Longarm demanded.

The barkeep, a large burly man with thinning hair oiled flat on his pale skull, shrugged. "Hell, mister, we got plenty of Valley Tan."

Longarm sighed. What had he expected? He was deep in Mormon country and Valley Tan was a Mormon drink. A first cousin to whiskey, it was brewed only in Utah. Tradition said it was made of fire and brimstone with the kick of an insane mule.

"That all you got?"

"That's it, mister."

Longarm shrugged. "All right."

Longarm paid the barkeep, and was heading for an empty table when two men pushed through the batwings and came to a halt in front of the flipping doors. The biggest and oldest was a squat, bowlegged fellow with a bulldog face and a belly that rode over his gunbelt. A town marshal's badge was pinned to his grease-stained vest. The young man beside him, evidently the town marshal's deputy, was a sun-scalded towhead with eager, vacant eyes.

The town marshal's glance caught Longarm at once. He heaved himself toward Longarm, his black button eyes gleaming, the deputy following along with him.

The town marshal halted in front of Longarm. "Guess you'd be the Custis Long just registered at the Palace Hotel."

"Glad you can read, Marshal."

His big face twisted into a mean grin. "You bet I can read. Too bad you can't run."

"Now why would I want to do that?"

"Because I'm lockin' you up."

"What for?"

"I got a warrant for your arrest, sworn out by Sheriff Gil Blowser. I'll be holding you until he gets here. You better come quiet."

"I'd like to see that warrant first."

"You can see it when I lock you up, mister."

"You're making a mistake, Marshal. I'm a lawman. A U.S. federal marshal."

"Prove it."

Longarm drew his wallet from his inside breast pocket and flashed his badge. The town marshal stepped closer to peer at the badge, then snatched it from Longarm.

"I don't believe you," the town marshal snarled. "You must've stole this from one of them federal marshals got himself shot out here. Hell, maybe you're the one been wipin' them out."

It didn't matter what he told the marshal, Longarm realized. The man was working hand in glove with Sheriff Blowser and his gang. Grinning at him, the town marshal drew his sixgun.

"Now just turn around, mister, and place both hands on the bar while I take your weapon."

Longarm turned around obediently. The bottle of Valley Tan was still on the counter. Longarm grabbed it,

95

swung around, and broke it against the side of the marshal's head. The marshal dropped his revolver and collapsed to the floor, the side of his face slamming heavily against the brass rail.

As Longarm stepped past the downed man and headed for the batwings, a sawed-off cue stick wielded by the barkeep caught him a glancing blow on the side of his shoulder, staggering him. Swinging around, Longarm reached over the bar and grabbed the barkeep around the neck, yanked him over the bar, and snatched the cue stick from him and hammered him on the head with it. The young deputy flung himself at Longarm and took a wild, futile swing at him. Ducking under the punch, Longarm clobbered the deputy in the face with the pool cue, exploding it.

Four bar patrons rushed him then, managed to twist the cue from his hand, and began pummeling him mercilessly. They slammed him back against the bar and in their eagerness to get at him, they were squealing like pigs at a feeding trough. Longarm twisted out of their grasp, picked up a chair, and broke it over an attacker's head. But the rest kept on coming. With his back braced against the bar, Longarm snatched up a chair rung and flailed out at them, his chair rung splattering noses, crunching into necks, and smashing ribs.

Bloodied and awed, those still standing edged back, giving Longarm a clear path to the door. He started for the batwings a second time, but a moment before he reached them, two men jumped him from behind, pinning his arms. Longarm twisted about and flung the men to the floor, but now he was away from the bar, completely surrounded. Another one caught him from behind, then another and another until he was borne down by sheer weight of numbers. Someone kicked him in the kidneys. A searing pain shot through him. As he sagged forward, another blow caught him in the ribs. He heard himself cry out in rage and fury as another sharp blow, this one from a gun barrel, sent him spinning off into oblivion.

The foul stench of raw whiskey breath brought Longarm around. His eyes still closed, he felt someone poking clumsily at his face as one would at a slab of raw steak. Longarm opened his eyes. The first thing he saw was the crumbling plaster of his cell wall and the barred window above his bunk. He turned his head and saw a grizzled old-timer bending over him, his yellow mustache drooping over his jaw, his watery blue eyes intent. Longarm pushed the old man away, swung his feet down off the bunk—and found that both ankles were hobbled by chains attached to a ring embedded in the wall behind him.

"Goddamn it!" he cried, yanking futilely on the chain.

The little man watched him warily, as if Longarm were a wild man about to go berserk. Longarm stared unhappily at him. His head spun from the blow that had rendered him unconscious; but it was not something he couldn't live with, and after what he had been through, he found that a comfort of a sort.

Squinting at the little man, he asked, "Who're you?"

"Doc Jenkins. I came in to see how bad you were hurt."

"All right. How bad am I hurt?"

"You got a swollen eyebrow and some bruises on your

face and back where you was kicked, but you don't seem to be hurt too bad."

"Easy for you to say."

Longarm reached into his inside coat pocket and found he still had his small pack of cheroots. "You got a match?" Longarm asked, biting off the end of a cheroot.

The doctor reached into his black bag and took out a tin of kitchen matches. Scratching the match to life, he lit Longarm's cheroot. Longarm took a few puffs, then handed the doc a cheroot. The doc took it gratefully and lit up. He appeared to be just a mite unsteady on his feet. He had no tie and his white broadcloth shirt was filthy, his black frock coat in need of a good cleaning and pressing.

"You sure you're a doctor?" Longarm asked.

The man glanced over his shoulder. "As a matter of fact, Mr. Long, I'm not."

"So how come the black bag?"

"I found it in a rooming house closet in Chicago. It had all I would need to start a practice."

"So you came out here to practice, hey?"

He smiled slyly. "You might say that."

"How long have I been unconscious?"

"Since last night."

"How late in the day is it?"

"It's just after dark."

"What about the town marshal?"

"Sykes? He's up and about. But the side of his head's got a real deep gash. The bandage makes it hard for him to wear a hat. To hear him tell it, that's my fault."

"What about the others?"

98

"The barkeep ain't yet regained consciousness."

"I'm sorry to hear that."

"He'll be all right. He's breathin' regular." The doc shook his head wonderingly. "It's sure amazing. I treated three busted heads, two sets of cracked ribs, and noses that'll never be the same. I figure one poor son of a bitch is going to spend the rest of his life walking with a limp." The doc chuckled. "And all you've got is a headache and some bruises. Those men would have been better off if they'd tangled with a grizzly bear."

"You wouldn't happen to know if Sykes has sent for Sheriff Blowser, would you?"

"Someone rode out an hour ago. Word is he's gone to find the sheriff."

"In that case, I need a file, Doc."

"Why?"

"You're a doctor, aren't you?"

"That's what I've become, I suppose."

"So be a doctor. Save my life. With a file I can cut through these manacles and break out of here."

"Then you're not a deputy U.S. marshal as you claimed?"

"Of course I am."

"Then why run away? All you have to do is explain things to the sheriff when he gets here. He'll see at once that this is just a misunderstanding, and the town marshal will have to free you."

"Doc, Sheriff Blowser is the leader of the gang been tearing up this territory—and your town marshal has long since thrown in with him."

"Sheriff Blowser? Leader of an outlaw gang?"

"Can you think of a better cover?"

99

"Why, no—I can't."

"It's not unusual. It's happened before. Ever hear of the Plummer Gang?"

The doc nodded. "Yes, I think I have. My God, this accursed land. I have come to believe it is populated almost entirely with blackguards and villains."

"Now, Doc, will you please bring me a file?"

"I have one with me," the doc said. He pulled a pearl-handled file from his bag and handed it to Longarm.

Longarm examined it, pleased. It was a nail file, but an unusually large one. It would do nicely.

"When you're finished with it," the doc said, "I must have it back."

"What do you use it for?"

"To file away the edge of bones on blasted toes. You'd be surprised how often the men around here shoot themselves in the foot."

"No, I wouldn't. Thanks, Doc. I'll drop the file down behind the bunk here. That be good enough?"

"It'll have to do, I suppose."

"After I'm gone, you can make some excuse for getting back in here."

The doc smiled ironically. "That won't be difficult. I am forced at times to spend a night in here. Too much Valley Tan, I am afraid."

Longarm pocketed the file. "Maybe you better get back to your other wounded now, Doc."

The doc nodded and called out to the jailer. An old cowpoke came out of the town marshal's office, unlocked the cell door, and swung it back to let the doc out.

"He's come to, has he, Doc?" the jailer asked, peering in curiously at Longarm as the doc moved past him.

"Yeah," Longarm told the jailer. "I'm wide awake—and hungry too."

"Too bad, mister," the old cowpoke said as he swung shut the cell door and locked it. "You already missed supper. But maybe I can rustle up something for you later."

"I'd appreciate it, old-timer."

Longarm lay down on the bunk and waited for the jailer and the doc to disappear into the town marshal's office. As soon as the door closed behind them, he drew his feet up onto the bunk and bent to the task of filing through the two padlocks fastening the manacles to his ankles.

About an hour later, Longarm was reclining back on his cot when the old man appeared with his supper. Longarm sat up on his cot as the jailer paused outside his cell to peer warily in at him. Then he unlocked the door and swung it open. Before entering the cell with the tray, he glanced over at the chain attached to the manacles on Longarm's feet. Satisfied Longarm was secure, he ventured into the cell and put the tray down on the stool alongside the slops bucket. Straightening, the old man glanced over at Longarm. Something in his manner alerted Longarm.

"What's up, old-timer?" Longarm asked him.

The man shuffled back out of the cell. "Looks like you got company comin.' "

"You mean Sheriff Blowser?"

"Yep."

The old man pushed the cell door shut and locked it, then hurried off down the hall. As soon as he closed

101

the office door behind him, Longarm went back to what he had been doing before the jailer appeared. Working swiftly, he finished filing through the padlock on his right ankle. He had already done the same to the one on his left ankle. Carefully, he stood up and shook free of the shackles enclosing his ankles, then walked over to the stool on which his supper rested. He was ravenous.

What he saw was a pile of kidney beans flanked by two large, still steaming dog turds. He dumped the tin plate's contents into the slops bucket, then lifted the mug of coffee and sniffed it, then threw the mug's contents into the slops bucket as well. He returned to his bunk, sat back down on it, and worked carefully to make it appear that his feet were still shackled.

This accomplished, he lay carefully back down to wait for someone to come for his food tray. Only a few minutes later, the deputy, his nose a swollen, purplish mess, walked down the hall and paused by Longarm's cell, the keys in his hand jingling merrily as he peered in through the bars. There was a nasty, shit-eating grin on his face.

"How do you feel?"

"The beans were delicious."

"How about them sausages?"

Longarm just turned his head and stared at him.

The deputy grinned. "A mite rank, weren't they?"

Enjoying himself immensely, the deputy unlocked the cell door and walked over to peer down at the tray and the coffee mug sitting on it. "How was the coffee?"

"Lousy."

"You mean you drank it?"

"Sure."

The deputy laughed out loud, his head rearing back. "Mister," he cried gleefully, "that was horse piss you drank!"

Longarm was off the bunk before the man could wipe the grin off his face, and with one terrible downward swipe of the length of chain in his fist, he floored the man. Another quick swipe and the deputy lost consciousness. The chain had made hardly a sound, and Longarm had caught the deputy's key ring before it struck the cell floor.

Longarm bent to examine the deputy. The man was out, his breathing regular, his face a fresh side of beef. Longarm dropped the chain onto his bunk, took the deputy's sixgun, and left the cell. He swung the door shut behind him and locked the deputy inside. Then he padded quietly down the hall, keeping on past the door leading out into the back alley. Flattening himself against the wall beside the office door, he found it slightly ajar, and was able to hear clearly what was being said in the office. One of the posse members was talking to Sykes. Burrel Wilson. There was no way to mistake his loud, raw voice as he barked at the town marshal.

"All you're gettin' is your usual split, Sykes," Wilson was saying. "And Gil won't like it one bit, you tryin' to shake him down for more."

"I figure he'll be glad to pay," Sykes insisted, "what with me bringing in this U.S. deputy marshal. I'll be handin' him to you on a silver platter. Besides, you got any idea what we had to go through to nail this bastard?"

"That ain't the point. We ain't payin' no more than you and the sheriff already settled on. Look at it this way, Sykes, the bigger your share, the smaller it is for the rest of us."

"All right. All right. How far out is Blowser? We'll let him settle this when he gets here."

"Ten miles, maybe more. We been pounding our butts for too long now, and the horses near gave out on us. I'm the lightest, so Gil gave me the best horse we had and sent me on ahead to make sure you got him. Now let's take a look. I want to spit in the son of a bitch's eye."

Longarm heard the squeak of a swivel chair and the clump of boots heading for the office door. Before they reached it, Longarm pushed the door open and stepped into the office, cocking the deputy's big Colt as he leveled it on the two men. Longarm was glad the old jailer was not in the office.

"Oh, Christ," Sykes said in some dismay. "He's loose."

Burrel Wilson's face went hard with sudden resolve. He took a quick step back and reached for his Colt. At the same time Sykes leaped for his desk and dove for cover behind it. Longarm paid no attention to Sykes as he drilled Wilson in his side. But Wilson had more courage than good sense and stayed upright, firing back at Longarm. Ducking low, Longarm planted a hole in the man's chest, this round knocking him straight back against the wall. A dead man this time, Wilson slid down the wall, his twitching fingers continuing to jerk on his double-action Colt, sending three more slugs slamming into the floor at his feet.

Sykes jumped up from behind the desk, his own gun blazing. Longarm flung himself out through the open doorway as the slugs tore into the doorjamb inches above his head. Longarm waited in the hallway, heard Sykes scrambling out from behind his desk, then stepped back into the open doorway and pumped two quick shots into the town marshal. The man stumbled backward, sat down heavily in his swivel chair, spun crazily, and dropped out of sight behind the desk, a lantern crashing to the floor beside him.

The gun battle was over, but the walls of the small office were still reverberating. At that very moment, Longarm figured, townsmen were probably rushing to investigate the gunfire. He pulled his cross-draw rig down from a wall peg, and found his Colt and his derringer and watch in a drawer under the rifle rack, cartridges for both beside them. His wallet was in the same drawer. He dropped the cartridges into his side pocket, checked both weapons, and found them still loaded.

He smelled smoke and turned. The floor behind the desk was blazing. The lantern Sykes had knocked over had set fire to the place. Even as he watched, flames roared up the wall behind the desk and raced across the ceiling.

Longarm took his Stetson off a peg and left the jail by the back door. Ducking past the outhouse, he trotted down the alley toward the hotel.

"Fire!" he cried. "Fire!"

At once from the street came answering cries:

"Fire! The jail's on fire!"

"Get buckets!"

Longarm heard the tramp of running feet. He kept on down the alley until he reached the rear of the hotel. Stepping up onto the narrow back porch, he pushed inside.

The back stairs were dark and narrow. No one was using them. He mounted them two at a time. On the top floor he found his room locked and remembered that when he went out, he had left his key with the desk clerk. He stepped back and broke the door's lock with a single savage kick. The door swung wide. He ducked into the room, closed the door, and strode over to the window to look down.

The entire jailhouse was on fire, a black plume of smoke billowing into the night sky, its underbelly livid from the flames below. Two long lines of men were passing buckets of water to one another in a desperate but futile effort to quell the blaze. And surging around these two bucket brigades was a large and growing crowd of townspeople, most of them running back and forth aimlessly, like ants whose hill some giant has just stomped.

He left the window, gathered up his gear, and hurried from the room and down the stairs.

Chapter 8

The hotel lobby was empty and the room clerk was not behind the desk. Everyone was outside, Longarm realized, either fighting the fire or watching it. He left the hotel, trotted across the street, and ducked into the livery. He had finished saddling the chestnut and was tying on his bedroll when he heard someone clearing his throat behind him.

Longarm turned to see the hostler entering the stable.

"Thought you were over there trying to put out the fire," Longarm told the hostler.

"A kid told me someone was in here," the hostler said. Then he stopped and peered narrowly at Longarm. "Say, ain't you the one the town marshal just arrested?"

"That's me," said Longarm, flipping him a cartwheel. He led the horse out of the stall and stepped up into the saddle. "Now get out of my way."

"Hey, look, mister, I ain't got no quarrel with you," the hostler said, stepping quickly to one side. "Only I think you ought to know. The county sheriff and his posse just rode in."

"Sheriff Blowser?"

"He's the county sheriff, ain't he?"

Longarm flipped the man another coin. "Much obliged."

Ducking his head low, Longarm turned the horse around and rode out through the rear of the stable into the corral. Leaning over, he opened the corral gate, rode out through it, and turned down the back alley, heading out of town. Back on the main street, passing the last building, he heard angry shouts behind him, followed by the sharp crack of rifle fire.

Longarm turned in his saddle and saw Blowser's posse bunched in front of the burning building wheeling their horses to take after him. Longarm chuckled. Blowser and his men could not have had time to acquire fresh mounts.

Slapping his chestnut's rump, he lifted it to a steady, ground-devouring lope and headed for the jagged line of mountains rearing ahead of him against the night sky— as good a place as any to make a stand.

At dawn, careful to leave tracks that could be followed easily, Longarm reached the badlands and entered a steep-walled canyon. He followed it until he made his noon camp beside the swift, icy stream slicing through it. Unsaddling his horse, he ate some of the jerky in his saddlebags, then leaned his head back against a boulder and peered up at the eternal snows that capped the peaks west of this sun-blasted land of canyons and sheer rock walls. Pulling his saddle over to use as a pillow, he closed his eyes and rested, lulled by the murmur of the stream beside him and the gentle cropping sound of the chestnut feeding on the grass close by the stream.

He rested, but did not sleep.

When he set out again, he kept to the middle of the stream, the swift water at times reaching clear to the chestnut's hocks. He was looking for hard ground, or an outcropping of caprock. He finally found a suitable ledge and guided the chestnut onto it. He kept his mount to a slow walk so its shoes would not chip the stone surface. When he reached a stand of scrub pine crowding the ledge, he guided the chestnut into the trees and traveling silently over the needle-carpeted ground, rode deep into the pines, gaining altitude steadily until he glimpsed through the trees above him the bright, sun-bleached wall of a massive sandstone ridge. Riding out of the pines, he rode along the base of the ridge for a quarter of a mile until he found a narrow game trail that would take him to the top of it. When he reached the rocky spine's summit, he reined in the chestnut to look at what lay ahead of him.

From the canyon floor, he had caught glimpses of this ridge, and saw now that it might indeed afford him a direct route back to the canyon's entrance. He rode back along the ridge until he broke out of a shallow patch of scrub pine and saw before him an unobstructed view of the vast scrubland over which he had traveled to reach the canyon, while just below him was the canyon's entrance.

Peering into the shimmering distance, he saw nothing. Not a single rider. Not a tree. Neither antelope nor deer. Nothing moved on the baked sun-blasted scrubland. For a while Longarm considered the possibility that Blowser might have given up the chase. He found that hard to believe, however. Blowser had kept Longarm from sending a telegram to Billy Vail, but he couldn't keep the lines down permanently. Blowser had to silence Longarm—and soon—if he and his gang were to survive.

Longarm unsaddled the chestnut and led it back to a grassy flat behind the pines. Then he poured some water from his canteen into the crown of his hat, enough to quench the horse's thirst for now, after which he went back through the pines with his rifle and settled down with his back to a pine to wait.

An hour later his patience was rewarded.

Like ants moving across a vast tablecloth, the six riders crept toward the canyon's entrance, following Longarm's tracks. They were strung out in single file, spaced far apart, an indication of how weary they and their mounts were. Longarm took up his rifle, left the trees, and angled carefully down the steep slope. About twenty yards below the ridge, he hunkered down behind a boulder and waited for the tiny figures on the flat below to enter the mouth of the canyon.

It took a while, but when they were all inside, Longarm took sight on the last of the riders. It was Hound, the one who didn't like cooking for his fellow gang members. Well, he wouldn't have to cook for them anymore.

Longarm squeezed the trigger. Hound slumped forward, then slid off his horse. The crack of Longarm's rifle shattered the canyon's late afternoon stillness, and the riders ahead of Hound instantly spurred their horses to a gallop. Longarm tracked the next closest rider—Tim O'Malley—and fired. He missed, the round whining off a rockface just above the outlaw. His cloak flying,

O'Malley vanished down the canyon after the sheriff and the others.

Longarm got to his feet and watched the dust settle back to the canyon floor. He now had five scorpions trapped in a bottle.

He checked his .44's load and his derringer's, cranked a fresh round into the Winchester, and climbed the rest of the way down. The slope was steep and treacherous, and it took a while for him to gain the canyon floor. Once he did, he moved cautiously along the base of the canyon's north wall until he caught sight of Hound.

The wounded outlaw had crawled over to the wall and was sitting up, his back propped against it. Longarm held up and checked for sign that any of Hound's companions might have ridden back for him. But he saw no one. They were not all that concerned about Hound, it appeared. Longarm started up again. Hound saw Longarm approaching him, but made no effort to move. Kneeling on one knee beside Hound, Longarm examined the gunshot wound. His Winchester's round had crashed into Hound's right shoulder and ranged down through his lungs to find a resting place somewhere in his gut. Hound's long hands were resting on his belly, his mournful face frozen in agony.

"Kill me, for Christ's sake," he murmured to Longarm. "Don't leave me here like this."

"You do that for them two marshals?"

"They died quick, so help me."

"Both of them?"

"I swear."

"I won't kill you, but I'll make it easy for you."

"How you goin' to do that?"

111

"Like this."

Longarm brought the barrel of his sixgun down hard on the top of Hound's head. Uttering scarcely a sound, Hound spilled loosely forward onto the sand, his hat falling off.

Longarm took the black, floppy-brimmed hat and exchanged it for his own Stetson. Then Longarm peeled Hound's ratty black duster off him and shrugged into it. Its trailing edges were caked with old mud and it stank like an abandoned privy, but Longarm wasn't going dancing in it. He stuck Hound's sixgun in his belt and looked around for the outlaw's mount. It was nowhere in sight, so he kept on afoot.

Rounding a bend in the canyon a few minutes later, he came on Hound's horse cropping the grass in a shaded spot close to the canyon wall. It was a big fat dapple gray. Longarm spoke to it softly as he approached, gentling it, then caught its trailing reins and vaulted into the saddle.

He spurred the horse out into the center of the canyon and rode deeper into it, keeping himself slumped awkwardly forward over his saddlehorn, as if he were Hound nursing a bad shoulder wound. He made sure that Hound's floppy-brimmed hat kept his face and neck in shadow. A quarter of a mile farther on, he rounded a bend and heard someone cry out from behind a patch of brush halfway up the canyon wall on the other side.

"Here comes Hound!"

Farther down, Tim O'Malley called out from behind a boulder. "You sure it's him?"

"Yeah, and it looks like he's been hurt bad."

"Hell, we knew that!"

Longarm pulled the dapple gray to a halt and glanced out from under his hat brim at the man halfway up the canyon wall—Will Coombs, his filthy red-and-gold serape pale with alkali dust, the gleam of his sixguns visible through the brush.

Bending even farther over the saddlehorn, as if he were about ready to pitch headlong from the saddle, Longarm urged the horse closer to Coombs.

"Hey, Hound!" Will Coombs called down to him. "You all right?"

It was a stupid question. Longarm didn't answer and rode closer.

"Hound!" O'Malley called. "What about Long? You see him?"

Again Longarm did not respond. At the foot of the canyon wall by this time, he slipped off the horse, then staggered a few steps up the trail leading to the patch of brush shielding Coombs.

"Hey!" cried O'Malley suddenly. "Watch out, Will. That ain't Hound!"

With no more need for playacting, Longarm flung off the stifling duster and charged up the path, his rifle in one hand, Hound's sixgun thundering in the other. The sixgun's slugs whipped through the brush, slamming into Will before he could return Longarm's fire.

Hit more than once, Will pitched forward through the brush and tumbled down the steep trail. Longarm saw Will's body cartwheeling straight for him, and braced himself an instant before Will crunched into him, then tumbled on past. The shock of the blow caused Longarm's feet to slip out from under him, and he had to fling himself flat on the steep slope to keep from following after Will.

As he sat up, a rifle shot from O'Malley plowed into the slope beside him, spitting clay and gravel up into his face. He flattened back down again and flung away Hound's empty sixgun. Squirming farther up the slope to a rocky outcropping, he took refuge behind it and brought up his rifle. Levering swiftly, he sent a fusillade down at the boulder behind which O'Malley was crouched. For a brief while, O'Malley made a halfhearted effort to return Longarm's fire, but soon Longarm heard above the whine of his ricocheting rounds the sudden clatter of hooves as O'Malley galloped off down the canyon. Longarm scrambled down to the canyon floor, mounted the dapple gray, and trotted after the fleeing outlaw. A half mile farther into the canyon, Longarm saw O'Malley's tracks as he rode across the stream and into a narrow draw.

Longarm followed the tracks cautiously.

As long as the tracks ahead of him were fresh, Longarm was not too worried about any bushwhacking attempt; and before long, the draw opened out onto a a grassy upland. Still following O'Malley's tracks, Longarm rode higher and higher until he entered a thick stand of timber. Here was where O'Malley would attempt to take him, Longarm realized.

He dismounted, and leading the dapple gray, kept after O'Malley, on the alert for trouble and beginning to wonder now about the sheriff and those other two bastards with him.

But one bastard at a time, he told himself.

Deep in the timber he caught a glimpse of O'Malley's horse through the trees and froze. After a little while,

he let go the reins of his own mount and circled widely around O'Malley's horse to come at it from the far
side. O'Malley was gone. Moving close to the horse,
Longarm noticed blood on the right stirrup. He had not
realized until this moment that his fusillade had wounded
O'Malley. However, O'Malley's wound could not have
been serious or the man would not have been able to
ride this far, this quickly.

Still, he was hurt and now—like Longarm—was afoot.

The forest floor was carpeted with pine needles and
left hardly a trace, either for a boot or a horseshoe. Not
knowing which direction to take, he circled the horse in
a gradually widening circle until he heard the thunder of
a distant waterfall and saw a patch of blue sky through
the trees. On a hunch, he headed for it, halting cautiously
just before he broke out of the timber. Peering through a
screening clump of saplings, he caught sight of O'Malley
crouched behind two boulders, his rifle held in readiness
on the ground in front of him, his one good eye scowling
through a coiling wisp of cigarette smoke. Not two yards
behind O'Malley yawned a deep gorge, trailing wisps of
mist from the pounding water below lifting into the air
behind him.

Longarm pulled back slowly and moved farther down,
making no more noise than a snake would tracking a
field mouse. Then he stepped out of the timber, his rifle
trained on O'Malley's head.

"Drop the rifle, O'Malley."

But O'Malley had glimpsed Longarm out of the corner
of his eye, and as Longarm fired, he jumped up and dove
into the timber. Longarm overtook O'Malley in the timber and tackled him from behind. O'Malley tried to fight

off Longarm, but after a few seconds, he groaned loudly and gave up the struggle. Longarm dragged O'Malley out of the timber. In the struggle, the outlaw had lost his eye patch, revealing the burnt-out hole in his skull. O'Malley's wound was in his right foot, and his boot had filled with blood. But the outlaw was game enough, his one good eye blazing defiance at Longarm.

"Go ahead, you bastard," he said. "Shoot me and be done with it."

Longarm took the man's Navy Colt from its tied-down holster and flung it into the gorge, then he picked up his rifle and trained it on O'Malley. He had no intention of shooting O'Malley, not that the man didn't deserve to get his brains blown out. Wounded as he was, Longarm figured he would have to take care of O'Malley and pack him back to civilization. If any of this ugly business came to a trial, he would make an excellent witness.

If he could be persuaded to cooperate, that is.

"Where are the others?" Longarm asked him.

"How the hell would I know? We split up."

"You think maybe the sheriff and those other two ran out on you?"

"I wouldn't put it past them. What're you goin' to do to me?"

"I been thinking about that."

"I'm hurt. Hurt bad. This here leg is shot all to hell. Why don't you just let me go?"

"Let you go?"

"Sure. With this foot wound I'm finished. I can't hurt you now."

"Now, why should I let you go, O'Malley?"

"Hell, I got nothin' personal against you. Why not?

116

Get the sheriff. He's the one you want."

"Them other two with him. Who are they?"

"Blowser's stepbrothers. Birds of a feather."

"You don't like 'em either, huh?"

"They always got a bigger share than any of us and they took less chances. Bloodsuckers, both of them."

"What a shame."

"Well, you goin' to let me go?"

Longarm stepped back. "Get to your feet."

"You know I can't do that. I'm hurt bad."

"I don't believe you."

Grudgingly, O'Malley tried to push himself upright, but as soon as he put any weight on his right foot, he collapsed forward onto the ground. Longarm grabbed his belt and heaved him upright. He had just about decided to bring the man in, and his intention at the moment was to help the wounded man to hobble back through the timber to his waiting mount. But the outlaw had other plans. He swung around with surprising alacrity, snatched Longarm's rifle, and twisted it out of his hand. Despite his shot-up foot, he hobbled swiftly away from Longarm and leveled the rifle on Longarm.

"You got healthy fast," Longarm commented.

Leaning back against a tree, O'Malley grinned, adjusting his torn, dusty cloak about his shoulders.

"Go ahead and reach for that .44," he told Longarm, grinning.

"Why don't you come over here and take it from me?"

"All right. Step closer so I can."

Longarm stepped to within a few feet of O'Malley. As the outlaw reached under the skirt of his frock coat and

117

lifted the .44 from its cross-draw rig, Longarm grabbed quickly for the rifle.

But O'Malley was way ahead of him. Laughing, he ducked back and swung the rifle's barrel like a club, catching Longarm on the side of the head. The force of the blow drove him to one knee. As Longarm shook his head to clear out the cobwebs, he was grateful that O'Malley had been too busy to see the bulge of his derringer in his fob pocket.

Watching him carefully, O'Malley tucked the .44 into his belt and cranked a fresh round into the Winchester, then stepped back, grimacing with the pain.

"Get up, you son of a bitch. I ain't finished with you yet."

Longarm got to his feet. "Pull the trigger then."

"I want to do it slow. I want you to think about it first."

"You going to use that rifle or talk me to death?"

"Turn around."

Longarm had been weighing the advisability of drawing his derringer. But he realized now what a hopeless play that would be with the Winchester trained on him.

O'Malley barked at him a second time. "You heard me, Long. Turn around."

Longarm turned.

"Now march. Straight ahead."

Longarm broke from the timber, O'Malley close behind.

"Keep going," O'Malley barked.

Longarm skirted the two boulders, kept on through a patch of brambles, their thorns catching at his pants, and came to a halt on the rim of the gorge. He could hear the dim thunder of the falls farther downstream. Below him—a long way below him—the swift mountain stream churned through the narrow gorge, clouds of water vapor hanging over it.

Longarm understood at once. They had never found the bodies of the two other deputy marshals or that Pinkerton. And now, if O'Malley had his way, they would not find his body either.

Longarm heard O'Malley slip the safety off the Winchester and without thinking any more about it, stepped out into space.

Chapter 9

Longarm hit the icy stream boots first. He struck close under the steep slope, his body knifing down through the water, his boots plowing into a pocket of deep sand the swirling current had created. He went to his knees and tumbled forward, nearly losing consciousness. But the water's viselike cold shocked him into wakefulness, and as he was swept along, his head emerged from under the surface. He gulped air, but before he could start stroking for the shore, the swift current pulled him under, sweeping him rapidly along just beneath the surface. For a punishing moment he was caught in a violent whirlpool, then flung out of it, only to be slammed against a huge boulder embedded in the streambed. He tried to grab hold of its wet, smooth surface, but the surging waters plucked him off it and swept him into a narrow channel that sliced through a steep sandstone cliff.

The current was deep and incredibly swift. As he struggled to keep his head above water, he heard a faint shot from overhead and a portion of the rock wall beside him exploded. At once he let the water pull him under and sweep him on through the channel. Once out of it, his progress became still swifter and not at all gentle as he skimmed over rocks, was sucked through narrow pools, and slammed constantly into sharp boulders, each time with brutal, numbing force. When he tried to regain some control, he found himself unable to muster the strength—and then suddenly he came to the downstream falls he had heard from above.

His speed increased, and then he found himself plunging almost straight down amidst a roaring wall of water. He began to tumble, but before he made a complete turn, he knifed into a deep churning pool at the base of the falls. This time the cold was paralyzing. A swift undertow caught him and dragged him deeper and still deeper into the icy waters. Abruptly, the buffeting ceased. But the cold seemed to have sapped him of all strength, and he made no effort to save himself as he began drifting down . . . down . . . turning lazily—like something completely spent.

Or dead.

The thought startled him and turning, he reached up and began to pull upward toward a distant, shimmering light. The pain in his oxygen-starved lungs was excruciating. Yet no matter how hard he struggled to reach that light playing on the surface so far above him, it grew no brighter, came no closer.

He seemed to be as far from it as when he first glimpsed it.

His right hand broke the surface, struck a rock crowding the stream, then brushed harshly against another. His body was dragged ruthlessly over sharp rocks, their edges digging at him and buffeting him cruelly. Then his head broke the surface and he found himself in a swift, shallow tributary. Sucking in deep lungfuls of air, he kept his head above the surface, and swam for the nearby bank. Clinging to a rock, he glanced back and saw the stream's main body roaring on past him. He glanced upward. The sheer, towering walls of the gorge almost shut out the light from the sky. It was toward this distant glow that he had struggled. No wonder it had seemed so impossible to reach.

Yet, if he had not tried to do so . . .

He shut off the thought and pulled himself out of the water, reminding himself as he did that O'Malley was still up there somewhere with his Winchester. Once on the pebbly shore, he pulled himself up a rough, steep trail until he found a shallow socket hollowed out of the cliff face, its entrance partially hidden by a clump of scrub pine. Squeezing past the pine, he slumped down wearily, his back against the rock.

Battered, weary, he took off his boots, emptied out the water, took off his cross-draw rig, his watch, and derringer. He held the watch up to his ear and was amazed to find it still ticking. Shivering in the high, thin air, he pulled off his boots, then his soaking clothes. He hung the clothes on the pine branches. His body was a mass of bruises. As he explored it with his hands, his fingers ran over welts and numerous bleeding wounds the sharp rocks had opened in his hide. There was a particularly long slash down his left thigh. The wound was clean, however, and would probably heal without scarring.

He was well above the stream now, the roar of the falls upstream a distant, almost tranquil sound. He glanced at the sky. It was close to sundown. The gorge was already deep in shadow. He drew his knees up under his chin and hugged them close to keep warm. Promising himself he would not sleep too long, he closed his eyes and dropped off immediately. When he opened them again, it was the cruel night chill that had awakened him. He was shivering so violently that, no matter how fiercely or diligently he clamped his jaw shut, he could not prevent his teeth from chattering. When he pushed himself upright, every bone, every muscle in his body protested the move. Peering through the scrub pine, he glanced up at the wedge of night sky visible above the walls of the gorge and saw no moon, only a sprinkling of gleaming stars. From their location, he knew morning was not far off. He shuffled painfully back against the rock wall, sat back down, and hugging himself again, prepared to wait for the blessed warmth of a new day.

Despite his trembling frame and chattering teeth, he slept.

Morning came with a clamor of bird song. His eyes snapping open, he peered again through the pine branches and watched a bright band of sunlight plant itself across the top of the rock wall opposite. He stood up, and found himself still pretty stiff but able to live with it. He plucked his still-damp clothes from the branches and, gritting his teeth against the awful chill, pulled them on. Then he checked his watch again. It was still ticking. He wound it gratefully and dropped it into his vest pocket, then checked his derringer.

The bird song above his ledge abruptly ceased. Beyond the pines a bird darted across his line of vision. He parted the pine branches carefully and peered down the slope. A one-eyed, cloaked horseman was riding up through the stream, keeping close to the shoreline, his head down as he looked for tracks.

O'Malley.

Longarm hunkered down and watched.

It wasn't long before O'Malley found the spot where Longarm had pulled himself from the water. He dismounted painfully, studied the ground carefully, then glanced up at the scrub pine, his one eye looking almost directly at Longarm. Even from this distance, the man's gaping eye socket was visible. As Longarm watched, O'Malley took a crude crutch and Longarm's Winchester from the saddle scabbard and limped toward the base of the slope. He started up the steep trail Longarm had taken and hobbled up it for a short way, then halted, braced himself on his crutch, and peered more carefully at the scrub pine. Longarm moved back as O'Malley hauled up the Winchester, then went flat. He was just in time as O'Malley began firing at the scrub pine.

Hugging the ground, Longarm cursed as the rounds sliced off branches and exploded pine cones over his head, then continued on to ricochet off the wall behind him. The fusillade stopped. Longarm lifted his head and peered through the pines, and saw O'Malley fling aside the empty Winchester. Longarm had flung O'Malley's Navy Colt into the gorge earlier. But O'Malley still had Longarm's .44.

"I know you're up there, Long!" O'Malley cried, hefting the revolver. "You couldn't have got far last night. Not in your condition. I'm coming up after you!"

"Come ahead," Longarm yelled. "I'll be waiting."

O'Malley did not hesitate as he hobbled up the steep

trail toward the pines. He wanted to get close enough to make sure of Longarm. The only rounds he had now were what remained in Longarm's .44. Longarm always rode with the hammer resting on an empty chamber so as not to blow a hole in his foot, which meant that O'Malley only had five more rounds.

Longarm had the two rounds in his derringer—something O'Malley knew nothing about.

"Hey, O'Malley," Longarm called down. "Why not let me ride out of here? Give us both a break."

"It's you needs the break. And I ain't givin' you none."

"Think it over, O'Malley."

"Hell, you shot up my foot. It ain't never goin' to be the same. I owe you. Besides, I hate lawmen."

"All right," Longarm replied grimly. "It's your call. Come ahead. I'm waiting."

O'Malley continued his dogged struggle up the trail. Longarm went down flat behind the scrub pine and kept his eyes on O'Malley as the man pulled himself closer, his face a mask of pain, sweat pouring down his face from the effort of dragging his shattered foot after him. He made for a grim, tenacious enemy.

A couple of feet below the pines, O'Malley flung up the .44 and squeezed off two quick shots, chewing up a branch and causing the wall behind Longarm to explode in rock shards. Longarm slammed his head down, his derringer in his fist. He wanted O'Malley to get closer before he used it. Then Longarm had a bright idea.

He groaned aloud, as if he had just been hit.

O'Malley bit and hobbled closer, raised the revolver, and punched two more shots into the pines. One slug passed so close to Longarm's right shoulder, it took a small piece of his coat with it.

Longarm stopped groaning and waited.

O'Malley still had a round left.

His head down, Longarm did not dare move as he picked up the sound of O'Malley's crutch dragging across the ground.

"How bad you hurt, Long?" O'Malley asked.

Longarm did not reply. O'Malley's voice had sounded pretty damn close, less than six feet from the pines. He heard O'Malley move still closer. Glancing up, Longarm saw the barrel of his .44 poking down through the branches less than three feet from his head.

O'Malley chuckled. "I see you, you bastard. You ain't dead—yet!"

Longarm reached up and grabbed the barrel, yanking hard. It exploded, the bullet slamming into the ground beside Longarm. O'Malley let go of the revolver and ducked back. Longarm burst out through the pines, his derringer blazing. The first bullet went over O'Malley's head, the second caught the outlaw in the side. He staggered and dropped his crutch.

But he was not done yet.

A huge bowie materialized in his right hand and with a furious snarl, he lunged wildly at Longarm. The knife flashed upward, catching Longarm's sleeve, but only grazing his arm. Again O'Malley thrust. But the man's wounds were too much for him. He was unable to put any weight on his foot, and the knife missed wildly. Longarm ducked aside and grabbed O'Malley's wrist with both hands. He twisted sharply. O'Malley gasped in pain and dropped the knife. He tried to kick it away with his one good foot, but Longarm snatched it off the ground and in the same upward sweep buried the bowie hilt deep into O'Malley's stomach.

"Oh, shit," O'Malley muttered.

He looked down at Longarm's bloody fist holding the blade deep in his gut.

"Go ahead, you bastard," he said. "Finish what you started."

Longarm ripped upward until he struck a rib, then pulled the blade free. He stepped back. O'Malley went over backward, blood gouting from his belly. He hit the slope hard, bounced slightly, then rolled back down the trail, coming to rest facedown in the water. Longarm kicked the dead man's crutch after him down the slope. It clattered loudly and came to a halt beside O'Malley's quiet body.

Longarm climbed down the steep slope and flipped O'Malley over onto his back to make sure the outlaw was dead, not that there could really be much doubt of it. The outlaw's one good eye was open wide, staring up at Longarm, his cruel, piratical face smeared with mud.

He was very much dead.

Longarm dragged the outlaw's body out to the main stream and kicked him into the water. The swift current plucked his body off the shore and swept it away. Longarm watched the dead man turn once, then sink beneath the surface.

He turned away.

Three more to go, he reminded himself wearily.

Close to sundown, his lanky frame as sore as a bronco-buster's at roundup, Longarm was back on the limestone ridge above the canyon's entrance. Easing himself back against a rockface, he chucked back his snuff-brown Stetson, which he had retrieved, and lit a fresh cheroot. The Winchester across his lap, he was waiting for the sheriff and his two relatives to pass beneath him on their way out of the canyon. The way Longarm figured it, without his gang at his back, Sheriff Blowser would be eager to get out of this canyon.

As shadows darkened the canyon floor below him, three riders clattered into sight. The sheriff was in the lead, his two companions riding side by side behind him. Longarm stood up, slipped off his safety, and fired a warning shot into the air.

"Hold it right there, Blowser!" Longarm called down.

The sheriff pulled up, startled.

"You too, Windy, Ely," Longarm shouted. "I'm taking the three of you in."

"Like hell you are," called Windy, drawing his sixgun.

Longarm fired a warning shot across Windy's saddlehorn, then levered a fresh round into the Winchester's firing chamber.

"Don't be a fool," Longarm warned. "I'll cut you down. Now drop them irons!"

"Hell, no!" cried Ely.

He drew his own sixgun and began blazing up at Longarm. Longarm did not bother to duck back as the rounds fell short, whining off the rocks at least twenty feet below him. At this distance, he was well out of range of a handheld Colt. He swung up the Winchester, sighted on Ely, and squeezed the trigger.

Nothing happened. Misfire.

Swearing, he cranked a fresh round into the gun, but

Ely was already spurring past the sheriff, heading for the canyon's mouth. Longarm tracked him hurriedly, fired, and missed. Encouraged by Ely's success, the sheriff and Windy galloped after him. Patiently, Longarm levered in a fresh round, tracked the sheriff, and fired.

A second after the stock bit into his shoulder, the sheriff slipped forward in his saddle, then hung on grimly as his horse carried him out of the canyon. Windy was a couple of horse lengths behind him. Longarm cranked the Winchester and considered whether or not to send a round after him. But why waste a bullet? They were now out of range.

He stood up. He felt very tired. Maybe he should have opened up without warning them. After all, what chance had this gang given their robbery victims—or those lawmen they'd assassinated? At least he had winged the sheriff. Blowser would need medical attention for his wound maybe, and since Iron City was his base, he was probably heading for it right now.

Longarm trudged wearily back to the chestnut, shoved his Winchester into its scabbard, then swung up into the saddle. He couldn't sling the chestnut onto his back and climb straight down to the canyon floor. He would have to retrace his route back along the ridge, and this would put him a good three hours or more behind the sheriff.

Which meant he could not expect a welcome reception when he did reach Iron City.

Chapter 10

It took Longarm much longer than he had counted on to reach the canyon floor, and it was dusk the next day when he rode into Iron City. As he entered the town, he kept himself alert, in case the sheriff had arranged a reception for him. What he found instead was that few of the townsfolk even bothered to glance up as he rode past.

Had the sheriff returned here? he wondered.

Longarm dismounted in front of the livery. Hoss appeared in the doorway, peering closely at him in the fading light.

"Hey," Hoss said, "ain't you the gent came in from the Osborne ranch and joined the sheriff's posse?"

"That's right, Hoss," Longarm said, leading the chestnut past the hostler into the barn.

"How come you didn't come back with him?"

"We got separated," Longarm replied, relieved to learn that the sheriff had indeed returned to Iron City.

"Oh," said Hoss.

"Where do you want my horse?"

Impatiently, the old cowpoke limped closer, took the chestnut's reins, and led it to a rear stall. Longarm followed in after the horse. He took off his gear and unsaddled the horse. He set the saddle down on top of the stall's partition. Stepping out of the stall, he told Hoss to give the chestnut an extra portion of grain and warned him to go easy on the water. Then he flipped Hoss a dollar.

As Hoss pocketed the coin, he cleared his throat. "Now, mister, ain't you goin' to tell me what in hell happened?"

"Happened? What are you drivin' at, Hoss?"

"Why, hell, the whole town's talkin' about it! The sheriff rode in with two strangers this afternoon and he had a bullet in him."

"You don't say."

"And his deputies and the posse that rode out with him was wiped out. Not a one came back."

"Except me."

"That's right. Except you. So what in blazes happened?"

"Maybe you better ask the sheriff."

"Ask him? He's hurt bad. And it's made him so ugly, he ain't talkin' to no one."

Longarm shrugged. "Sorry, Hoss. It's his story. You better let him tell it."

"Well, what about them two rode in with him?"

Longarm hefted his bedroll onto one shoulder and slung his saddlebags over the other one. "You mean Ely and Windy?"

"That their names?"

"That's right, Hoss. They're the sheriff's stepbrothers."

Hoss let fly with a gob of chewing tobacco. "Step-brothers, hey? You mean they was born of a woman? I figured they'd crawled out from under a damp rock."

Longarm took up his Winchester and strode from the livery. Crossing the street to the hotel, he registered and lugged his gear up to his room. Dumping it onto his bed, he left the hotel and walked down the street to the barbershop, where he soaked himself inside a metal tub for a good hour, then got himself a shave and a haircut.

Unaware that Longarm was one of those who had ridden out with the sheriff, the barber did not ply him with questions as had Hoss. Instead, he talked a blue streak, and as Longarm lay back, the hot towels steaming open the pores on his face, he learned that when the sheriff rode in he had refused to talk to anyone as his brothers pulled him off his horse and helped him up the steps to the doctor's office over the undertaker's parlor.

The doctor was not in his office, so Ely and Windy went looking for him. They found him in a nearby saloon and hauled him out into the street. When he protested, they belted him into submission and dragged him up to his office. This display of brutality outraged everyone in town, and the barber related the incident to Longarm in hushed, angry tones.

Longarm listened silently, and when the barber peeled off the sheet and snapped off the cuttings, Longarm paid the man without comment. He left the shop and walked down the main street, looking for the undertaker's parlor. When he reached it, he glanced up at the doctor's office on the second floor. A light glowed in the windows, so he mounted the steps, rapped once on the door, then stepped into the office.

It was empty. So was the treatment room beyond it. Longarm hurried back down the steps and crossed the street to the Iron City Saloon. Pushing inside, he halted to look about the smoky interior for the doctor, and caught sight of a rawboned man in a derby hat gloomily nursing a half-empty shotglass at a table in the rear. A black leather doctor's bag sat on the floor beside his chair.

Longarm strode through the crowd and halted by the man's table. The fellow glanced quizzically up at Longarm. There was a raw-looking bruise under one eye, and Longarm recalled the barber's account of how he had been manhandled.

"Guess you'd be the doctor," Longarm said.

"I am."

"Mind if I join you?"

"Sit down. You buying?"

"Sure."

The doc waved over a bar girl. Longarm ordered a shot of Valley Tan. The doctor ordered the same. The girl left.

"You got a name, mister?"

"Long. Custis Long."

"What's your problem?" the doc asked. "You look pretty healthy to me—except for some scratches on your face. But then a healthy woman could've done that."

"Is that what happened to you—a woman?"

"Not quite."

Their drinks arrived. Longarm batted his down. The doctor picked up his shotglass and sipped the poison, then waited for Longarm to tell him what he wanted.

"I just visited your office to get the sheriff. He wasn't there."

"I fixed the son of a bitch and kicked him out. He's gone to his room at the Mormon Rest, a boardinghouse down the street, him and his two brothers."

"The two gorillas, you mean."

"Yes."

"How bad was Blowser wounded?"

"All he had was a slug in the meaty part of his back, near the right shoulder blade."

"Can he use a weapon?"

"With his left hand, maybe."

"He can travel now?"

"Sure. He wasn't hurt all that bad." The doc grinned suddenly. "I took my time when I dug the slug out, and I didn't give him anything for the pain. The big slob was bawling like a baby when I finished."

"You sound like you enjoyed it."

"I did."

"So he's at the Mormon Rest now."

The doc nodded, then cocked his head and peered at him quizzically. "You the one winged him?"

"How could you tell?"

"The sheriff couldn't keep his mouth shut. From what I gathered, you're a U.S. deputy marshal and you're the one that's been stalking him."

"And now I'm about to finish it."

"Tell me something."

"Sure."

"Is there any chance this bastard was the leader of that gang that's been raising hell around here?"

"There is."

"Where's his gang now?"

"I wouldn't worry about them now."

The doctor leaned back and studied Longarm shrewdly. "I see."

Longarm got up. "Guess I'll go visit the Mormon Rest now and pick up the bastard. Where is it?"

"Three blocks. On your right. But if I was you, I'd watch out for them two with him."

"I will."

"Maybe you're hoping they do give you trouble."

"You could say that."

Longarm dropped a coin on the table to pay for their drinks and left the saloon.

The door to the Mormon Rest was opened by a tall, gaunt, formidable woman in her fifties with a mustache. She was in a black housedress, carried herself like a soldier, and fixed him with a steely glance.

"If it's a room yer lookin' for, mister, we're full up."

"I've come to visit with the sheriff," Longarm said.

"He's hurt bad. I don't think he wants any visitors."

"It's official business, ma'am."

"Who're you?"

Longarm reached for his wallet and flashed his badge.

"Oh," she said.

She stepped back and he stepped into the entry hall.

"Sheriff Blowser is upstairs with his brothers. They've taken the first two rooms at the head of the stairs."

Longarm thanked her and started up the stairs. When he heard the owner of the rooming house enter the kitchen below, he unholstered his .44, knocked softly on the door at the head of the stairs, and waited. There was no answer to his knock.

He knocked a second time, then tried the door. It was not locked. He pushed it open and stepped into the doorway, then halted. The room was a mess. It looked as if someone had ransacked it—either that or left in one hell of a hurry.

"Custis . . . ? Is that you?"

Longarm swung around to see an amazed and delighted Matty Keefer standing not ten feet from him in the hall. He holstered his Colt and peered at her in some astonishment. She looked as fresh and chipper as a bird in springtime, and was dressed in a red lounge robe with a plunging neckline. From the way it clung to her ample body, he realized that once again she was wearing nothing under it.

"However did you find me?" she gasped.

Before he could muster a reply, she flung herself into his arms, planting her lips over his with great enthusiasm. When they parted, he stepped back from her, making no effort to hide his pleasure at finding her in this rooming house.

"Matty, what are you doing in Iron City?"

"You mean you didn't know I was here? You didn't come after me?"

"Matty, I had no idea you were here."

Longarm heard the iron tread of the housekeeper below them. She was heading for the foot of the stairs, evidently anxious to investigate the voices on the landing.

"We can't talk out here," he told her. "Where's your room?"

She took his hand and pulled him eagerly down the hall and into her room. She closed the door and leaned back against it, smiling warmly at him. "I don't care why you're here. I'm just so glad to see you!"

"Me too, Matty. You going to tell me what happened?"

"I left Walter."

"That's a pretty drastic move, isn't it?"

"He left me a long time ago, when he became so wrapped up in his new young wife." She shrugged. "And then he found himself another one. So I took his flatbed and the team and drove back here."

"Why here?"

She smiled. "Charlie Webb."

"Who's the hell's he?"

"The handsome gentleman who owns the general store. When Walter stopped on our way through to purchase some provisions, I could tell Chuck took a shine to me."

Longarm sagged onto her bed, immensely relieved. "So now you and him have an understanding. That it?"

"We will have. He's calling for me later this evening."

"I hope the two of you will be very happy."

"Oh, I'm sure we will. Just so long as he ain't no Saint."

"Who is?"

She smiled and dropped to the bed beside him. "But that don't mean you and me have to act like perfect strangers, does it?"

"I guess not," he said with a grin.

She peeled off her robe and flung it over her shoulder. Longarm heard it hit the wall. His guess had been on target. The only thing she was wearing under the robe was her birthmark.

"Now, just a minute, Matty."

"Don't be bashful. Get your coat and shirt off while I pull down your britches."

"I hate to say this, Matty, but I just don't have the time."

But she didn't pay any attention to his protests as she flung her arms around his neck and kissed him eagerly, her tongue thrusting boldly as her hand reached down for his crotch. He could feel her fingers struggling to unbutton his fly. Laughing throatily, she rolled over onto him. Despite his preoccupation with the sheriff and his eagerness to get after him, he found himself getting aroused.

"Oh, I just can't wait, Custis," she cried. "Please help me with your fly!"

"First," he said, "I got some questions, Matty."

She sat back on the bed, her generous breasts bouncing slightly, her hand squeezing him where it did the most good.

"Questions?" she asked. "What questions?"

"About the sheriff. I thought he was rooming here."

"He was, and you can just imagine how surprised he was to see me here. He almost fainted, but I told him I wouldn't shoot at him again."

As she spoke, her fingers finally managed to get his fly all the way open. "Oh, my," she said, as her fingers found his soaring erection.

Doing his best to ignore her ministrations, he said, "The sheriff's not here now. Where is he?"

"He rode out with the other two."

"When was this?"

"A little after dusk."

"You sure? You saw them ride out, did you?"

"Yes, I did."

Longarm stood up quickly. She let go of his engorged member, and experiencing some difficulty, he buttoned up his fly.

"Longarm," she pouted. "What's wrong? Where are you going?"

"After the sheriff."

"But I'm so *ready* for you."

"Save it for Charlie then."

Longarm clapped on his hat. "Now, Matty, can you tell me which way they went?"

"South."

"You sure of that?"

She nodded emphatically. "I was in the kitchen when they rode out. They kept their horses in the alley back of the house here. I watched them from the kitchen window."

"What were you doing down there?"

"Mrs. O'Riley was shopping and asked me to look after the house for her. I was in the kitchen making coffee."

"Then she doesn't know they've left?"

"I didn't tell her. I didn't tell anyone, until now."

"Did you hear what they planned, anything like that?"

"They're on their way back to Texas."

"Texas?"

"And they're hoping to make the River Bend stage depot before midnight."

He grinned at her. "You heard a lot, Matty."

"They were real loud and they didn't know I was in the kitchen. I made sure to keep out of sight."

She got up from the bed and pressed herself hard against him. He was genuinely sorry he didn't have more time.

"I really have to go now, Matty."

"I know," she said, sighing. "I remember you told me you were after them. Do you think they saw you ride in?"

"I've just about figured that's what happened."

There was a sudden, seductive gleam in her eyes. She thrust herself still closer. He could feel the hot scent of her breasts as they pressed against him.

"Couldn't you stay for just a little while longer?"

"The trouble is, I wouldn't want it to be for just a little while, Matty."

"You're a terrible man. And I'll miss you. Be careful, Custis."

"I will, Matty."

He took her face in his hands and kissed her on the lips, then turned and left her standing naked before her bed. He hoped Charlie would be able to handle what was in store for him.

It was mid-morning when Longarm caught sight of the stage's way station in the distance. He had been unable to give the chestnut enough time to recover, with the result that he had had to go slow the night before. The last thing he needed now was for the chestnut to founder.

The way station was a low log building with barns and corrals surrounding it. There was a stream behind it, and in the pastures on the other side of it Longarm could see the stage line's horses grazing. In the corrals behind the barn, the stationmaster was leading a fresh team of horses into the barn.

As Longarm rode into the yard, he glimpsed the stationmaster's wife lugging two buckets of water into the way station. She scarcely glanced at him as she disappeared into the building. Longarm dismounted and walked into the horse barn to greet the stationmaster.

He was sweating as much as the horses he was backing into the stalls. Longarm waited until he had managed to back the biggest of the horses into its stall. Finished with that chore, the stationmaster strode toward him, mopping his face and neck with a red bandanna.

"Who are you, mister?"

Longarm showed him his badge. "Custis Long. I'm a U.S. deputy marshal. You got a few minutes?"

"That's about all I got. There's a stage due here in less than half an hour."

"You had some guests last night?"

"I did."

"Sheriff Blowser and two others?"

The stationmaster walked past Longarm out into the yard. "May!" he called.

His wife appeared in the doorway, drying her hands on her apron. "Yes?"

"Bring that letter!"

She vanished back inside.

"What's this about a letter?" Longarm asked.

"The sheriff left it for you. He said you'd probably be coming by here lookin' for him."

Longarm saw the stationmaster's wife leave the way station with the letter in her hand.

"Then Sheriff Blowser's already ridden on."

"Yep. Course, that don't mean he's goin' to get where he's goin'."

"What do you mean?"

142

"The way he treats his horse. That mount he's pushin' isn't liable to get too much further. Not in this heat."

"Didn't you tell him that?"

"No one tells that bastard anything."

"Which way did he go. South?"

"Nope. Southwest. He's headin' for Rim Rock."

"All three?"

"Nope. His sidekicks went in the other direction."

His woman had reached them by that time. Shading her hands against the sun, she handed the letter to her husband.

"Here," said the stationmaster, passing it on to Longarm—apparently well pleased to be rid of the chore. "The sheriff was sure anxious for you to get this."

The letter was just a dirty, folded piece of paper sealed with candle wax. Opening it, Longarm found a barely legible scrawl in pencil that read:

Long,
    We no all about yer rancher frends. And that girl what patched you up. Maybe you shud see if she is all rite now, fore you waste time chasin me.
                                        Gil Blowser

With an angry cry, Longarm crumpled the note and flung it aside. *The sheriff had sent Ely and Windy after Ruth!*

For a moment he had difficulty breathing. He felt as if he had been kicked in the stomach.

Without a word to the stationmaster, he hurried out of the barn, vaulted into his saddle, pulled the chestnut around, and headed out of the yard. He could not help

143

recalling what those two animals had done to that settler's place—and to the settler. The recollection almost made him groan aloud.

He leaned forward over the chestnut's neck and despite the heat urged it to a full gallop.

Chapter 11

Ben pushed open the door. "Rider comin'!"

Ruth hurriedly put down the pot she was scouring and ran to the door to peer out. The sun's glare was such that she could not see the rider without shading her eyes with her hand. Even so, the rider was still so far from the cabin that he was little more than a wavering, shimmering figure as he rode toward them through the heat.

Her first thought was that it was Custis, alive and well, coming to say good-bye to her before returning to Denver. Jim appeared in the doorway beside her. No longer needing to carry his arm in a sling, he was beginning to fill out nicely.

"Think it might be Custis?" he asked, reading her mind.

She glanced eagerly at him. "That's what I was hoping."

"Me too."

Behind them, Ben said, "We better rustle up some coffee. You still got any of them doughnuts left, Ruth?"

She laughed and turned to him. "I've got plenty."

"Let's not count our chickens before they're hatched," said Jim.

He was frowning now as he peered more closely at the oncoming rider. Ruth looked more closely at the rider as well. The heat waves were not breaking up horse and rider as much as before. The man rode with his body bent forward over his horse, and his face was not visible, so low was the man's hat brim. Beside her, Jim reached for the shotgun leaning against the wall by the doorway.

"That ain't Custis," he said warily.

"No, it isn't," Ruth agreed.

"I don't like his look."

"Is he at all familiar to you?"

"Nope. Never saw him before. But that don't matter. I still don't like the look of him."

Jim broke open the shotgun, loaded it, and snapped it shut. He looked back at Ruth's father. "Forget the coffee and doughnuts, Ben. Get out your iron and stay out of sight in the bedroom."

"Why, mebbe he's just a stranger ridin' by."

"He ain't ridin' by—he's coming straight for the ranch. He's got business here, I think."

Ben took his sixgun out of the top drawer in the sideboard and ducked into the bedroom. Jim stepped up beside Ruth in the doorway. The rider was clearly visible now. He was a short, squat fellow who rode atop the saddle, it seemed, not in it. He was wearing a battered derby hat and a filthy, sheepskin coat that appeared to be in tatters.

"Jim, I think I know that man," said Ruth, frowning suddenly, her voice betraying her fear.

"Who is he?"

"I don't know. What I meant was, he fits the description Custis gave of one of the two men who tried to kill him before you came on him."

"You sure?"

"No, how could I be?"

"Well, he looks like trouble, sure enough. Get in back of me. I'll handle this."

She started to argue, then caught herself and stepped behind Jim, peering over his shoulder as the rider kept on into their yard and pulled his mount to a halt in front of the ranch house.

"Howdy, mister," he said to Jim, his smile a yellow one.

"Howdy."

"Just ridin' by. Saw your place. Like to light and rest a while, maybe gulp down a cup of coffee. It's been a long day for me."

"Water your horse at the trough," Jim told him coldly. "And we'll send out some coffee."

"That ain't very neighborly."

"It's the best we can do," Jim said. "We got sickness in the house. Best for you to stay out here."

Slowly the man dismounted, lifted his ruin of a derby to wipe off his forehead, then stretched like a filthy animal just emerging from a hole in the ground—only Ruth had never seen any animal as dirty as this man. Starting toward them, he smiled, his face a mask of alkali dust and grime.

"Hold it right there," Jim said. "Nobody's invited you in."

"You goin' to shoot down a stranger? In cold blood?"

"I'll do what I have to do. Maybe you better forget about that cup of coffee. Get back on your horse and ride out."

"Couldn't do that. My mount's about ready to give out."

"That's not my problem."

The man, still smiling, kept coming. "Well, then, maybe you could sell me one of your mounts. I'll even throw in this here horse as part of the deal."

Jim released the shotgun's safety. "I told you to get back on that horse, mister. One more step and I'll blow your balls out through your ass."

The man pulled up, his face suddenly distorted. "You son of a bitch." he snarled. "You would do that, wouldn't you."

"Yes, I would. Now turn around and ride out of here."

Ruth heard a boot scuffing the floor behind her, whirled, and saw a tall man stepping through the cabin's back door. He had a nervous, crazed look about him, and was raising the gun in his hand to fire into Jim's back.

She screamed.

Her father rushed from the bedroom, his Colt in his hand. The lanky stranger swung his gun around and fired point-blank at Ben, the force of the slug knocking the old man back into the bedroom. At the sound of Ruth's scream, Jim had whirled, and Ruth heard him being struck down from behind, his shotgun clattering against the doorsill.

But all she could think of was her father.

"Pa!" she cried, rushing toward the bedroom. "Pa!"

As she flung herself down beside him, she heard the tall one chuckling. "That old son of a bitch is a gone beaver, lady. And you will be too, if you don't calm down."

Horrified, she looked up at the man.

"You heard me. So wait nice and quiet for that friend of yours to show up, that deputy U.S. marshal."

The other rider walked into the cabin and stood beside his companion. He was carrying the shotgun. "You give us any trouble and we'll finish off your friend back there."

"You hear that?" the taller one demanded, his rasping voice raw with menace.

Numb with grief, Ruth nodded, then looked back down at her father. His eyes were open wide in pure astonishment, a thin trickle of blood coming from his mouth. His shirtfront was darkening ominously.

"I'm all right, kitten," Ben whispered. "It don't hurt bad. It's like someone punched me, that's all."

Scalding tears coursing down her cheeks, Ruth brushed her father's white hair back off his forehead and nodded hopefully.

Ben closed his eyes and died.

Bound and gagged, sitting up with her back against the wall near the front door, Ruth had plenty of time to consider her situation. And to ask herself nervously how badly Jim had been hurt by the blow that had knocked him out. He had been flung in the corner beside the kindling box, his hands bound behind him. He was only partially conscious, and every once in a while he'd groan softly. Was this her fault? she wondered. Perhaps if she hadn't screamed out like that, he wouldn't have turned and exposed his back to that first rider.

149

And Ben would not have rushed out of the bedroom.

There was a terrible, yawning emptiness inside of her whenever she allowed herself to recall the loss of her father. And meanwhile, she could not keep the tears from her eyes. The two men had dumped Ben's body outside on the ground near the privy; then they had dragged her into the bedroom and flung her down on her bed, where they had taken their pleasure, rutting like the wild, filthy creatures they were.

She had taken it as well as she could by closing her eyes and telling herself that this awful violation was happening not to her, but to someone else; her real self was not involved. Yet now, whenever she let down her guard, the horrid ugliness of it would sweep over her, filling her with a shuddering revulsion.

She wondered bleakly if she would ever be clean again.

When Ben burst in to tell her of the approaching rider, she had been making bread, and though she had rinsed then wiped her hands on her apron, she had been too excited to do a very thorough job. As a result, she had almost been able to pull her left wrist free of the rope binding it. With the one called Ely glancing back at her constantly from his post at the window, she did not dare struggle too openly, lest he get curious and decide to check the rope binding her.

At last she managed to pull her wrist all the way through the rope. In a moment both hands were free. Keeping them out of sight behind her, she began flexing her hands to restore their circulation. The pins-and-needles sensation this aroused was so painful she almost cried out. But she uttered not a sound, kept both hands behind her back, and kept her eyes on Ely.

The outlaw was still kneeling beside the window. His brother was outside in the barn loft, waiting to fire on Custis from the hay-loading door. Their plan, which neither made any effort to conceal from her, was for Ely to show himself in the doorway with Ruth at his side when Custis rode up. The two men figured he would be too concerned for Ruth's safety to think to look behind him as he rode into the yard. Ely would get him to dismount, then both men would both open up on him.

Ruth shuddered at the thought, and told herself she must not let that happen!

Beside the kindling box, Jim groaned and stirred fitfully. Ely glanced irritably over at him, then looked at Ruth. She struggled fitfully so he would think she was still securely bound. Again Jim groaned. Ely got up, went over to Jim, and kicked him brutally until his head sagged forward. Then Ely walked over to her, reached down, and shoved the towel he was using as a gag still farther down her throat. Ruth gasped and fell back, tears flooding her eyes. This reaction seemed to make Ely feel a whole lot better. Smiling, he went back to the window.

Watching him carefully, Ruth began to wind the rope loosely back around her wrists so that when he pulled her upright to stand in the doorway, he would still think her hands were securely bound.

She wanted it to be a surprise when he found out otherwise.

It was late in the afternoon when Longarm came in sight of the Osborne ranch. The sun was at his back, and he knew that anyone in the ranch house could see him coming. He kept the barn between him and the cabin for as long as he could. He had no doubt the two were waiting for him. And that they would use Ruth for a shield, a bargaining chip to get him close enough to finish him off.

The trouble was, he did not see how he could do anything else but ride up, bargain for her release, and hope for some kind of a break that would maybe narrow the odds some in his favor. But no matter what, he must not let any harm come to Ruth.

He left the barn's shadow and in full sight of the ranch house rode directly for it. Once he rode in past the gate, the door was flung open and Ely appeared. Longarm reined in the chestnut. As Longarm had expected, a bound and gagged Ruth was propped up in the doorway beside him. She looked like she'd been through hell, and from the temper of those two, he knew she probably had. He did not like to think of what they had already done to her.

But she was alive.

For Ely to have shown himself this soon meant that he was a mite overanxious. Longarm pulled his chestnut to a halt, trying to figure where Jim and Ben were. He assumed Windy was at the front window on the other side of the doorway, covering his brother.

Or maybe he was in the barn. But how could he find that out for sure?

Still on his horse, Longarm called, "Let her go, Ely."

"Why should I?" the man shouted back.

"It's me you want."

"Ride closer then," Ely told him, releasing Ruth and taking his rifle in both hands and aiming it at Longarm.

Ely hadn't shot Longarm already, Longarm realized, because he wanted to make his first shot count, and at that distance, he was not sure he could.

"Send her out here," Longarm yelled, "so she can take my horse and ride out."

Ely didn't like arguing. He grabbed Ruth and pulled her closer, then jabbed his rifle barrel hard against her face. Longarm saw Ruth flinch away as the cold metal dug into her cheek.

"You heard me," Ely shouted. "Move in closer, I said. And do it now, or I'll blow this girl's brains into the next county."

Longarm spurred his horse on into the yard. The threat was real and he could not afford to bargain any longer, not with Ruth's life at stake. As he rode to within thirty yards of the cabin, however, Ruth suddenly straightened up and spun away from Ely.

"It's a trap!" she shouted, her hands loose and pounding at the startled Ely. "The other one's behind you in the barn loft!"

Longarm drew his sixgun and turning his horse sharply, galloped straight for the barn. He saw Windy's rifle poking down through the hay and before the outlaw had a chance to aim and fire, emptied his .44 into the hay behind it. With a despairing cry, Windy plunged forward out of the loft. He landed on the top of his head, crunching down onto the hard-packed ground with awesome force. Longarm wheeled his horse and, his rifle out of its scabbard now, charged full-tilt back toward the house.

Ruth was still struggling with Ely in the doorway, both hands on his rifle. With the ferocity of an aroused she-

153

cat, she was doing her best to wrest the weapon from Ely's grasp. Suddenly the rifle discharged and Ruth fell back. She was unhurt, but the rifle's detonation had been enough of a shock to shake her loose from it. But Ely had no time now to crank a new shell into the rifle's firing chamber. He flung the rifle away and drew his sixgun.

Longarm leaped from his horse and bowled into Ely, driving him back through the open doorway into the cabin. The man stumbled and went down under Longarm's furious charge. Somehow he managed to hold on to his revolver. Rolling away from Longarm, he flung it up. On one knee, Longarm fired his rifle, levered, and fired a second time. His first round blew Ely's face apart, his second dug a neat hole in his filthy shirt.

As quickly as that it was over.

Chapter 12

"You sure you don't want me to side you?" Jim asked.

"Thanks, Jim," Longarm replied. "I appreciate it. But you still got some mending to do, judging from that gash on your head. I'd prefer it if you'd stay here and give Ruth a hand. She'll be all alone now."

Jim glanced at the somber woman—no longer the tigress that had tried to wrest the rifle from Ely Smith's hands.

"I don't mind stayin', not if she don't."

"You know how I feel about that, Jim," she replied, smiling at him.

It was her first smile since Longarm rode in.

The three of them were sitting at the kitchen table. It was dusk. After the shootout, they had dumped the sheriff's brothers into a shallow grave behind the barn, close by a small mountain of horseshit. Then they had taken the body of Ruth's father out to a birch-crowned hill overlooking the ranch. The service for Ben had been sim-

155

ple and moving, with Ruth reading the old man's favorite psalms from the family bible.

"Do you have to ride out so soon?" Ruth asked Longarm.

"Yes, Ruth."

"But it'll soon be dark."

"I don't want the sheriff to get too far ahead of me."

"Do you expect much trouble?" Jim asked.

"Not with his brothers out of the way and him wounded."

"You'll stay for a good supper," Ruth said.

It was not a question, but a statement that brooked no refusal. She got up from the table, walked over to the stove, and began shoving fresh kindling into it.

"Is that an order?" Longarm asked with a smile.

She returned his smile. "I won't have it any other way."

"Then I won't either."

As Ruth busied herself preparing their supper, Longarm watched Jim's eyes as they followed her movements; he saw reflected in them a concern and affection for her that would soon ripen into love—if it had not already done so.

Good. He was leaving Ruth in good hands.

The next afternoon, when Longarm saw ahead of him on the trail the half dozen or so buzzards feeding on a horse's carcass, he recalled the stationmaster's remark on how poorly the sheriff took care of his horse. Once abreast of the grisly banquet, Longarm dismounted, took off his hat, and waved it at the buzzards. Flapping their great wings, the gorged birds ran a few ungainly feet to gain momentum, then launched themselves reluctantly into the searing air.

Walking closer to the lather-flecked, gaping remains of the horse, Longarm kept his eyes peeled for boot prints leading away from it. He found them and followed them on foot, keeping after them until they veered off the trail into the badlands. He peered up at the tangled land of rock and shrub looming before him, then walked back to his horse and swung aboard it. Following the single set of tracks left by the sheriff, he turned off the trail and proceeded into the badlands, wishing as he rode that Blowser had been able to make it to Rim Rock. He was as dry as a rain barrel in August; in Rim Rock there were places where a man could wet his whistle.

It was dusk when Longarm saw the blazing campfire ahead of him, and realized it was serving more as a signal fire than a campfire. Longarm dismounted and circling widely, approached the camp from a ring of rocks above it. When he peered down at the camp, he saw Blowser sitting on a log close to the fire, a blanket wrapped around him as he hugged himself and rocked miserably in the frigid desert night.

He was waiting for his brothers to arrive, no question. It would be a very long wait.

His rifle held ready, Longarm left the rocks and picked his way down the slight slope leading to the camp. He was only a few feet from it when Blowser caught the scuff of Longarm's boot heel against a rock and spun around. He had a sixgun in his hand.

"Hold it right there, Blowser," Longarm warned him. "You're covered. If you don't want me to send another bullet into you, drop the gun."

"Damn you!" the sheriff cried.

He tossed the revolver to the ground. Longarm moved swiftly to the man's side, snatched the weapon up, and stuck it into his belt. Then he leaned his rifle against a boulder, stepped closer to the fire, and gazed down at the sheriff.

"Thought you were heading for Texas," Longarm said.

"I am. Later."

"You mean you were. You can forget about Texas, Blowser. I'm bringing you in. Yuma is about as close as you're going to get. If they don't hang you, that is."

"Didn't you get that note I left for you?"

"I got it."

The sheriff's face lost its color. For a moment he didn't understand. Then he did. "But, my brothers . . . didn't they . . . ?"

The grim smile on Longarm's face stopped him.

Longarm nodded coldly. "That's right, Blowser. They're both dead. The trouble is they took a decent man with them."

"Ely, Windy—dead?"

"You heard me."

"My God. You wiped us all out!"

"There's still you left to go."

"Now, listen here, Long. Just wait a goddamn minute! I've got money! You don't think I've had a chance to spend what I took, do you? We can split it between us! Fifty-fifty."

"Fifty-fifty?"

"All right! Sixty-forty. You get sixty percent. All I want's the rest."

"Where you got this money?"

"You remember that shack in Skull Canyon? It's not

so far from here. I buried the money in a steel trunk in back of the privy. There's at least twenty thousand in it, I tell you. A fortune!"

It was at that. Frowning, Longarm appeared to consider Blowser's proposition. Then he shrugged.

"Okay. You lead the way."

"We can leave in the morning," Blowser cried eagerly.

"I'll sleep back up there in the rocks," Longarm told him. "I warn you. Don't try anything. I sleep light."

"Hey, we're partners now. Don't worry. Besides, where am I going? I don't have a horse. And I'm wounded."

"That's right. So you are."

Longarm turned and trudged back up into the rocks. He waited until Blowser had fallen asleep, then trudged back to his horse, rode a half a mile farther into the badlands, made a dry camp, and slept.

No sense in sleeping that close to a rattlesnake.

A good hour after daybreak, completely refreshed after an undisturbed night's sleep followed by a hearty breakfast, Longarm peered down at Blowser's abandoned camp. The sheriff was gone. He'd left his partner behind.

Longarm smiled. He was pleased—but not surprised—that he had guessed right.

He let his horse pick its way down the rocky slope to the campsite and dismounted. A quick look about the dead fire told Longarm that most likely the sheriff had fled soon after Longarm disappeared in the rocks the night before. He followed the clear track left by Blowser as he'd dragged himself and his bedroll along, keeping himself as close to the ground as possible until he'd felt it was safe for him to get to his feet and take off.

Longarm returned to his horse and rode after Blowser, doing nothing to increase his horse's pace, content to stay on the man's trail. In due course, he knew, he would overtake the fleeing man. He did so a little before noon, the sun overhead like a branding iron.

His back leaning against a boulder about two hundred yards distant, Blowser had come to rest. His rifle lay on the ground in front of him, the barrel reflecting the sun's merciless glare. Longarm dismounted, left his horse, and keeping low, moved forward. Crouching behind a tangle of brush, he sighted carefully and put a round into the ground about ten feet in front of the sheriff.

The man flung himself flat, snatched up his rifle, and peered into the glare, searching for Longarm. Longarm levered and put another round in among the rocks just behind the sheriff. The sheriff jumped up and started running. In a moment he had disappeared in among towering rock forms and twisting canyons.

Longarm stood up, brushed himself off, returned to his horse, and dropped his rifle back into its scabbard. Mounting up, he urged his horse to an amble as he kept on after the sheriff, alert for any attempt at an ambush. When he came to a stream two hours later, he saw where Blowser had slogged hurriedly across it. Longarm did not ride straight for the stream, however, but scouted both banks for at least a quarter of a mile in each direction. Finding no sign of the sheriff forting up to bushwhack him, he dismounted, led his horse to the stream, and let it drink its fill, then filled both canteens. He stripped then and took a dip in the water. After a short meal, he napped, mounted up again, and continued after the sheriff, completely refreshed.

By mid-afternoon, the sheriff's tracks were getting easier and easier to follow. The man was keeping to open country, making a beeline for that shack in Skull Canyon. Only it wasn't exactly a beeline anymore. The man was staggering. And in spots Longarm could see where he had crawled into the shade of trees or an overhanging rock wall to get out of the sun's crushing rays.

When Longarm overtook him again, Blowser had propped himself up against a canyon wall about a hundred yards farther on. It was obvious the sheriff was waiting for him. He had given up trying to escape Longarm or beat him to the shack. He was too far gone for such tricks now.

Longarm stepped down off his horse, led it into the cover of some rocks, then snaked his Winchester from its scabbard. He walked forward until he was within seventy yards of the sheriff, then made himself comfortable on the ground. Taking his time, he tucked the rifle's stock into his shoulder, sighted carefully, and squeezed the trigger. Thirty feet in front of the waiting sheriff the ground erupted.

Blowser waved his hand desperately. He could not see Longarm, and craned his neck in an effort to pick him out among the rocks. Longarm could hear his faint voice calling out. The sheriff was insisting that he was ready now to be taken in, that he was through running.

Sure, you are, Longarm muttered to himself as he aimed carefully, then placed another slug about twenty feet in front of the sheriff.

Then ten feet.

His fourth shot whined just over the frantic sheriff's head.

Blowser turned and ran for his life. Longarm stood up and watched him go until he was out of sight.

Then he went back for his horse.

Wheeling buzzards gave the sheriff's position the next time. It was late in the afternoon, and if anything, the sun seemed hotter than it had been at any time during the day.

Longarm turned his horse toward the circling birds, noting that as yet not one bird had dropped below the horizon. They were content, it seemed, to glide in great circles high above the sun-blasted badlands—like massive cinders caught in a bonfire's updraft. But there was no question the birds had their eyes on a possible feast below them.

Longarm soon found himself riding over a scrub-covered plateau, a twisting canyon lost in shadow below him. He kept on, recognizing some of its features, and realized he was riding along the rim of Skull Canyon. When he finally came in sight of the shack on a shelfland below him, he found that he was almost directly under the circling buzzards. Dismounting, he peered over the rim and found the sheriff sprawled flat on his back on a ledge about thirty feet below the canyon rim.

In his haste to reach the shack, Blowser must have tried to climb down the steep slope and lost his footing.

"Help me!" the sheriff cried. "I'm hurt bad!"

"Why should I?"

"You're a lawman! You got to help me."

"Did you help those two marshals—or that Pinkerton?"

"You leave me here it's murder."

"I'll get a rope."

Longarm went back to his horse for his lariat and returned to the canyon rim. He uncoiled the rope and dropped one end of it down onto the ledge to a spot close by the sheriff. Still flat on his back, the man made a feeble attempt to grab the rope, but was unable to do so.

"My back's broke," Blowser cried. "I can't move.!"

"I'll come down."

Longarm hauled the rope back up, tied it to a pine, then lowered himself down onto the ledge. He was bending over the prostrate sheriff when the man abruptly uncoiled. Jumping up onto his feet, he lunged for Longarm. Longarm sidestepped easily. Blowser vaulted out into space and twisting slowly—his scream filling the canyon—dropped into the canyon's shadows and vanished. The scream ended abruptly.

Longarm glanced up at the buzzards. They were still circling, but maybe they were a bit lower now.

Vail brought his beer and Longarm's over to the booth.

"How long you been here?" he asked, sliding into the seat and pushing Longarm's drink over to him.

"I just got here."

"That's good. I had some paperwork to finish at the office. You know how that is."

"What's this news you got for me?"

"Thought you'd like to know," Vail said with a pleased smile. "Wells Fargo found the money. It was right where you said it was. In a steel trunk behind the privy."

"I'm glad to hear it."

"There's something else."

"Oh?"

"The sheriff lied to you."

"That's hard to believe, Billy."

"There was forty-five thousand in that trunk, not twenty."

"Like he said, a fortune."

"The best thing is, Wells Fargo is so damn happy, they want to give you a portion of it as a reward."

"Not me. Divide it up among the survivors of those two marshals."

"What about the Pinkerton?"

"His too."

Vail was pleased. "He had a wife and a kid, I heard. I'll bet they can use it."

"It's settled then. Tell Wells Fargo."

"I already did."

Longarm shrugged and sipped his beer. "Did they find the bodies of the two marshals yet, or the Pinkerton?"

"No. But they sure as hell found a lot of other bodies— what the buzzards left of them, that is. The Wells Fargo men wanted to know if you were really alone on this assignment."

"You might say I was lucky."

"Damn lucky, from what you told me." Vail leaned back against the seat and cocked his head at Longarm. "There's just one thing I can't quite get clear in my head, Longarm."

"What's that?"

"You say when you lowered yourself onto that ledge to get Sheriff Blowser, you had a feeling he was going to try something. How the hell could you know that?"

"He told me his back was broken. He couldn't move, he said. But he was never hurt as bad as he let on, and when I lowered the rope to him, he made some feeble passes at it."

"So you knew he was not hurt as bad as he said."

"That's right, Billy."

"Then why in hell did you climb down onto that ledge to save him?"

"Billy, you got it all wrong."

"What do you mean?"

"I didn't climb down there to save him."

Vail frowned. "You didn't?"

"Nope."

It took a while for Vail to get it. Then he straightened up. "Oh," he said.

Longarm leaned back and sipped his beer.

"Now you got it," he said.

Watch for

LONGARM AND THE RAILROAD TO HELL

151st in the bold LONGARM series
from Jove

Coming in July!

GILES TIPPETTE

**Author of the best-selling WILSON YOUNG
SERIES, BAD NEWS, and CROSS FIRE
is back with his most exciting
Western adventure yet!**

JAILBREAK

Time is running out for Justa Williams, owner of the Half-Moon Ranch in West Texas. His brother Norris is being held in a Mexican jail, and neither bribes nor threats can free him.

Now, with the help of a dozen kill-crazy Mexican *banditos*, Justa aims to blast Norris out. But the worst is yet to come: a hundred-mile chase across the Mexican desert with fifty *federales* in hot pursuit.

The odds of reaching the Texas border are a million to nothing . . . and if the Williams brothers don't watch their backs, the road to freedom could turn into the road to hell!

*Turn the page for an exciting preview of
JAILBREAK by Giles Tippette*

On sale now, wherever Jove Books are sold!

At supper Norris, my middle brother, said, "I think we got some trouble on that five thousand acres down on the border near Laredo."

He said it serious, which is the way Norris generally says everything. I quit wrestling with the steak Buttercup, our cook, had turned into rawhide and said, "What are you talking about? How could we have trouble on land lying idle?"

He said, "I got word from town this afternoon that a telegram had come in from a friend of ours down there. He says we got some kind of squatters taking up residence on the place."

My youngest brother, Ben, put his fork down and said, incredulously, "*That* five thousand acres? Hell, it ain't nothing but rocks and cactus and sand. Why in hell would anyone want to squat on that worthless piece of nothing?"

Norris just shook his head. "I don't know. But that's what the telegram said. Came from Jack Cole. And if anyone ought to know what's going on down there it would be him."

I thought about it and it didn't make a bit of sense. I was Justa Williams, and my family, my two brothers and myself and our father, Howard, occupied a considerable ranch called the Half-Moon down along the Gulf of Mexico in Matagorda County, Texas. It was some of the best grazing land in the state and we had one of the best herds of purebred and crossbred cattle in that part of the country. In short we were pretty well-to-do.

But that didn't make us any the less ready to be stolen from, if indeed that was the case. The five thousand acres Norris had been talking about had come to us through a trade our father had made some years before. We'd never made any use of the land, mainly because, as Ben had said, it was pretty worthless and because it was a good two hundred miles from our ranch headquarters. On a few occasions we'd bought cattle in Mexico and then used the acreage to hold small groups on while we made up a herd. But other than that, it lay mainly forgotten.

I frowned. "Norris, this doesn't make a damn bit of sense. Right after supper send a man into Blessing with a return wire for Jack asking him if he's certain. What the hell kind of squatting could anybody be doing on that land?"

Ben said, "Maybe they're raisin' watermelons." He laughed.

I said, "They could raise melons, but there damn sure wouldn't be no water in them."

Norris said, "Well, it bears looking into." He got up, throwing his napkin on the table. "I'll go write out that telegram."

I watched him go, dressed, as always, in his town clothes. Norris was the businessman in the family. He'd been sent down to the University at Austin and had got considerable learning about the ins and outs of banking and land deals and all the other parts of our business that didn't directly involve the ranch. At the age of twenty-nine I'd been the boss of the operation a good deal longer than I cared to think about. It had been thrust upon me by our father when I wasn't much more than twenty. He'd said he'd wanted me to take over while he was still strong enough to help me out of my mistakes and I reckoned that was partly true. But it had just seemed that after our mother had died the life had sort of gone out of him. He'd been one of the earliest settlers, taking up the land not long after Texas had become a republic in 1845. I figured all the years of fighting Indians and then Yankees and scalawags and carpetbaggers and cattle thieves had taken their toll on him. Then a few years back he'd been nicked in the lungs by a bullet that should never have been allowed to head his way and it had thrown an extra strain on his heart. He was pushing seventy and he still had plenty of head on his shoulders, but mostly all he did now was sit around in his rocking chair and stare out over the cattle and land business he'd built. Not to say that I didn't go to him for advice when the occasion demanded. I did, and mostly I took it.

Buttercup came in just then and sat down at the end of the table with a cup of coffee. He was near as old as Dad and almost completely worthless. But he'd been one of the first hands that Dad had hired and he'd been kept on even after he couldn't sit a horse anymore. The problem was he'd elected himself cook, and that was the sorriest day our family had ever seen. There were two Mexican women hired to cook for the twelve riders we kept full time, but Buttercup insisted on cooking for the family.

Mainly, I think, because he thought he was one of the family. A notion we could never completely dissuade him from.

So he sat there, about two days of stubble on his face, looking as scrawny as a pecked-out rooster, sweat running down his face, his apron a mess. He said, wiping his forearm across his forehead, "Boy, it shore be hot in there. You boys shore better be glad you ain't got no business takes you in that kitchen."

Ben said, in a loud mutter, "I wish you didn't either."

Ben, at twenty-five, was easily the best man with a horse or a gun that I had ever seen. His only drawback was that he was hotheaded and he tended to act first and think later. That ain't a real good combination for someone that could go on the prod as fast as Ben. When I had argued with Dad about taking over as boss, suggesting instead that Norris, with his education, was a much better choice, Dad had simply said, "Yes, in some ways. But he can't handle Ben. You can. You can handle Norris, too. But none of them can handle you."

Well, that hadn't been exactly true. If Dad had wished it I would have taken orders from Norris even though he was two years younger than me. But the logic in Dad's line of thinking had been that the Half-Moon and our cattle business was the lodestone of all our businesses and only I could run that. He had been right. In the past I'd imported purebred Whiteface and Hereford cattle from up North, bred them to our native Longhorns and produced cattle that would bring twice as much at market as the horse-killing, all-bone, all-wild Longhorns. My neighbors had laughed at me at first, claiming those square little purebreds would never make it in our Texas heat. But they'd been wrong and, one by one, they'd followed the example of the Half-Moon.

Buttercup was setting up to take off on another one of his long-winded harangues about how it had been in the "old days" so I quickly got up, excusing myself, and went into the big office we used for sitting around in as well as a place of business. Norris was at the desk composing his telegram so I poured myself out a whiskey and sat down. I didn't want to hear about any trouble over some worthless five thousand acres of borderland. In fact I didn't want to hear about any troubles of any kind. I was just two weeks short of getting married, married to a lady I'd been courting off and on for five years, and I was mighty anxious that nothing come up to interfere with our plans. Her name was Nora Parker and her daddy owned and run the general mercantile in our nearest town, Blessing. I'd almost lost her once before to a Kansas City drummer. She'd finally gotten tired of waiting on me, waiting until the ranch didn't occupy all my time, and almost run off with a smooth-talking Kansas City drummer that called on her daddy in the harness trade. But she'd come to her senses in time and got off the train in Texarkana and returned home.

But even then it had been a close thing. I, along with my men and brothers and help from some of our neighbors, had been involved with stopping a huge herd of illegal cattle being driven up from Mexico from crossing our range and infecting our cattle with tick fever which could have wiped us all out. I tell you it had been a bloody business. We'd lost four good men and had to kill at least a half dozen on the other side. Fact of the business was I'd come about as close as I ever had to getting killed myself, and that was going some for the sort of rough-and-tumble life I'd led.

Nora had almost quit me over it, saying she just couldn't take the uncertainty. But in the end, she'd stuck by me. That had been the year before, 1896, and I'd convinced her that civilized law was coming to the country, but until it did, we that had been there before might have to take things into our hands from time to time.

She'd seen that and had understood. I loved her and she loved me and that was enough to overcome any of the troubles we were still likely to encounter from day to day.

So I was giving Norris a pretty sour look as he finished his telegram and sent for a hired hand to ride it into Blessing, seven miles away. I said, "Norris, let's don't make a big fuss about this. That land ain't even crossed my mind in at least a couple of years. Likely we got a few Mexican families squatting down there and trying to scratch out a few acres of corn."

Norris gave me his businessman's look. He said, "It's our land, Justa. And if we allow anyone to squat on it for long enough or put up a fence they can lay claim. That's the law. My job is to see that we protect what we have, not give it away."

I sipped at my whiskey and studied Norris. In his town clothes he didn't look very impressive. He'd inherited more from our mother than from Dad so he was not as wide-shouldered and slim-hipped as Ben and me. But I knew him to be a good, strong, dependable man in any kind of fight. Of course he wasn't that good with a gun, but then Ben and I weren't all that good with books like he was. But I said, just to jolly him a bit, "Norris, I do believe you are running to suet. I may have to put you out with Ben working the horse herd and work a little of that fat off you."

Naturally it got his goat. Norris had always envied Ben and me a little. I was just over six foot and weighed right around a hundred and ninety. I had inherited my daddy's big hands and big shoulders. Ben was almost a copy of me except he was about a size smaller. Norris said, "I weigh the same as I have for the last five years. If it's any of your business."

I said, as if I was being serious, "Must be them sack suits you wear. What they do, pad them around the middle?"

He said, "Why don't you just go to hell."

After he'd stomped out of the room I got the bottle of whiskey and an extra glass and went down to Dad's room. It had been one of his bad days and he'd taken to bed right after lunch. Strictly speaking he wasn't supposed to have no whiskey, but I watered him down a shot every now and then and it didn't seem to do him no harm.

He was sitting up when I came in the room. I took a moment to fix him a little drink, using some water out of his pitcher, then handed him the glass and sat down in the easy chair by the bed. I told him what Norris had reported and asked what he thought.

He took a sip of his drink and shook his head. "Beats all I ever heard," he said. "I took that land in trade for a bad debt some fifteen, twenty years ago. I reckon I'd of been money ahead if I'd of hung on to the bad debt. That land won't even raise weeds, well as I remember, and Noah was in on the last rain that fell on the place."

We had considerable amounts of land spotted around the state as a result of this kind of trade or that. It was Norris's business to keep up with their management. I was just bringing this to Dad's attention more out of boredom and impatience for my wedding day to arrive than anything else.

I said, "Well, it's a mystery to me. How you feeling?"

He half smiled. "Old." Then he looked into his glass. "And I never liked watered whiskey. Pour me a dollop of the straight stuff in here."

I said, "Now, Howard. You know—"

He cut me off. "If I wanted somebody to argue with I'd send for Buttercup. Now do like I told you."

I did, but I felt guilty about it. He took the slug of whiskey down in one pull. Then he leaned his head back on the pillow and said, "Aaaah. I don't give a damn what that horse doctor says, ain't nothing makes a man feel as good inside as a shot of the best."

I felt sorry for him laying there. He'd always led just the kind of life he wanted—going where he wanted, doing what he wanted, having what he set out to get. And now he was reduced to being a semi-invalid. But one thing that showed the strength that was still in him was that you *never* heard him complain.

He said, "How's the cattle?"

I said, "They're doing all right, but I tell you we could do with a little of Noah's flood right now. All this heat and no rain is curing the grass off way ahead of time. If it doesn't let up we'll be feeding hay by late September, early October. And that will play hell on our supply. Could be we won't have enough to last through the winter. Norris thinks we ought to sell off five hundred head or so, but the market is doing poorly right now. I'd rather chance the weather than take a sure beating by selling off."

He sort of shrugged and closed his eyes. The whiskey was relaxing him. He said, "You're the boss."

"Yeah," I said. "Damn my luck."

I wandered out of the back of the house. Even though it was nearing seven o'clock of the evening it was still good and hot. Off in the distance, about a half a mile away, I could see the outline of the house I was building for Nora and myself. It was going to be a close thing to get it finished by our wedding day. Not having any riders to spare for the project, I'd imported a building contractor from Galveston, sixty miles away. He'd arrived with a half a dozen Mexican laborers and a few skilled masons and they'd set up a little tent city around the place. The contractor had gone back to Galveston to fetch more materials, leaving his Mexicans behind. I walked along idly, hoping he wouldn't forget that the job wasn't done. He had some of my money, but not near what he'd get when he finished the job.

Just then Ray Hays came hurrying across the back lot toward me. Ray was kind of a special case for me. The only problem with that was that he knew it and wasn't a bit above taking advantage of the situation. Once, a few years past, he'd saved my life by going against an evil man that he was working for at the time, an evil man who meant to have my life. In gratitude I'd given Ray a good job at the Half-Moon, letting him work directly under Ben, who was responsible for the horse herd. He was a good, steady man and a good man with a gun. He was also fair company. When he wasn't talking.

He came churning up to me, mopping his brow. He said, "Lordy, boss, it is—"

I said, "Hays, if you say it's hot I'm going to knock you down."

He gave me a look that was a mixture of astonishment and hurt. He said, "Why, whatever for?"

I said, "*Everybody* knows it's hot. Does every son of a bitch you run into have to make mention of the fact?"

His brow furrowed. "Well, I never thought of it that way. I 'spect you are right. Goin' down to look at yore house?"

I shook my head. "No. It makes me nervous to see how far they've got to go. I can't see any way it'll be ready on time."

He said, "Miss Nora ain't gonna like that."

I gave him a look. "I guess you felt forced to say that."

He looked down. "Well, maybe she won't mind."

I said, grimly, "The hell she won't. She'll think I did it a-purpose."

"Aw, she wouldn't."

"Naturally you know so much about it, Hays. Why don't you tell me a few other things about her."

"I was jest tryin' to lift yore spirits, boss."

I said, "You keep trying to lift my spirits and I'll put you on the haying crew."

He looked horrified. No real cowhand wanted any work he couldn't do from the back of his horse. Haying was a hot, hard, sweaty job done either afoot or from a wagon seat. We generally brought in contract Mexican labor to handle ours. But I'd been known in the past to discipline a cowhand by giving him a few days on the hay gang. Hays said, "Boss, now I never meant nothin'. I swear. You know me, my mouth gets to runnin' sometimes. I swear I'm gonna watch it."

I smiled. Hays always made me smile. He was so easily buffaloed. He had it soft at the Half-Moon and he knew it and didn't want to take any chances on losing a good thing.

I lit up a cigarillo and watched dusk settle in over the coastal plains. It wasn't but three miles to Matagorda Bay and it was quiet enough I felt like I could almost hear the waves breaking on the shore. Somewhere in the distance a mama cow bawled for her calf. The spring crop were near about weaned by now, but there were still a few mamas that wouldn't cut the apron strings. I stood there reflecting on how peaceful things had been of late. It suited me just fine. All I wanted was to get my house finished, marry Nora and never handle another gun so long as I lived.

The peace and quiet were short-lived. Within twenty-four hours we'd had a return telegram from Jack Cole. It said:

YOUR LAND OCCUPIED BY TEN TO TWELVE MEN STOP CAN'T BE SURE WHAT THEY'RE DOING BECAUSE THEY RUN STRANGERS OFF STOP APPEAR TO HAVE A GOOD MANY CATTLE GATHERED STOP APPEAR TO BE FENC-ING STOP ALL I KNOW STOP

I read the telegram twice and then I said, "Why this is crazy as hell! That land wouldn't support fifty head of cattle."

We were all gathered in the big office. Even Dad was there, sitting in his rocking chair. I looked up at him. "What do you make of this, Howard?"

He shook his big, old head of white hair. "Beats the hell out of me, Justa. I can't figure it."

Ben said, "Well, I don't see where it has to be figured. I'll take five men and go down there and run them off. I don't care what they're doing. They ain't got no business on our land."

I said, "Take it easy, Ben. Aside from the fact you don't need to be getting into any more fights this year, I can't spare you or five men. The way this grass is drying up we've got to keep drifting those cattle."

Norris said, "No, Ben is right. We can't have such affairs going on with our property. But we'll handle it within the law. I'll simply take the train down there, hire a good lawyer and have the matter settled by the sheriff. Shouldn't take but a few days."

Well, there wasn't much I could say to that. We couldn't very well let people take advantage of us, but I still hated to be without Norris's services even for a few days. On matters other than the ranch he was the expert, and it didn't seem like there was a day went by that some financial question didn't come up that only he could answer. I said, "Are you sure you can spare yourself for a few days?"

He thought for a moment and then nodded. "I don't see why not. I've just moved most of our available cash into short-term municipal bonds in Galveston. The market is looking all right and everything appears fine at the bank. I can't think of anything that might come up."

I said, "All right. But you just keep this in mind. You

are not a gun hand. You are not a fighter. I do not want you going anywhere near those people, whoever they are. You do it legal and let the sheriff handle the eviction. Is that understood?"

He kind of swelled up, resenting the implication that he couldn't handle himself. The biggest trouble I'd had through the years when trouble had come up had been keeping Norris out of it. Why he couldn't just be content to be a wagon load of brains was more than I could understand. He said, "Didn't you just hear me say I intended to go through a lawyer and the sheriff? Didn't I just say that?"

I said, "I wanted to be sure you heard yourself."

He said, "Nothing wrong with my hearing. Nor my approach to this matter. You seem to constantly be taken with the idea that I'm always looking for a fight. I think you've got the wrong brother. I use logic."

"Yeah?" I said. "You remember when that guy kicked you in the balls when they were holding guns on us? And then we chased them twenty miles and finally caught them?"

He looked away. "That has nothing to do with this."

"Yeah?" I said, enjoying myself. "And here's this guy, shot all to hell. And what was it you insisted on doing?"

Ben laughed, but Norris wouldn't say anything.

I said, "Didn't you insist on us standing him up so you could kick him in the balls? Didn't you?"

He sort of growled, "Oh, go to hell."

I said, "I just want to know where the logic was in that."

He said, "Right is right. I was simply paying him back

183

in kind. It was the only thing his kind could understand."

I said, "That's my point. You just don't go down there and go to paying back a bunch of rough hombres in kind. Or any other currency for that matter."

That made him look over at Dad. He said, "Dad, will you make him quit treating me like I was ten years old? He does it on purpose."

But he'd appealed to the wrong man. Dad just threw his hands in the air and said, "Don't come to me with your troubles. I'm just a boarder around here. You get your orders from Justa. You know that."

Of course he didn't like that. Norris had always been a strong hand for the right and wrong of a matter. In fact, he may have been one of the most stubborn men I'd ever met. But he didn't say anything, just gave me a look and muttered something about hoping a mess came up at the bank while I was gone and then see how much boss I was.

But he didn't mean nothing by it. Like most families, we fought amongst ourselves and, like most families, God help the outsider who tried to interfere with one of us.

LONGARM

Explore the exciting Old West with
one of the men who made it wild!